```
792.02                  416370
Wil                     15.95
Williamson              Feb88
Behind the scenes
```

	DATE DUE		

GREAT RIVER REGIONAL LIBRARY

St. Cloud, Minnesota 56301

BEHIND THE SCENES

BEHIND THE SCENES:

THE UNSEEN PEOPLE WHO MAKE THEATER WORK

By

WALTER WILLIAMSON

Walker and Company
New York, New York

Copyright © 1987 by Walter Williamson

All rights reserved. No part of this book may be reproduced or transmitted in any form or by any means, electronic or mechanical, including photocopying, recording, or by any information storage and retrieval system, without permission in writing from the Publisher.

First published in the United States of America in 1987 by the Walker Publishing Company, Inc.

Published simultaneously in Canada by Thomas Allen & Son Canada, Limited, Markham, Ontario.

Library of Congress Cataloging-in-Publication Data

Williamson, Walter.
  Behind the scenes.

  Includes index.
  Summary: Reveals the work involved in theater through profiles of ten people active in various phases of the field, from playwright, producer, and general manager to master electrician, wardrobe master, and production carpenter.
  1. Theater—Juvenile literature. 2. Theater—Production and direction—Juvenile literature. [1. Theater—Production and direction] I. Title.
PN2037.W55 1987   792'.02   86-33981
ISBN 0-8027-6703-6
ISBN 0-8027-6704-4 (lib. bdg.)

Printed in the United States of America

10 9 8 7 6 5 4 3 2 1

Book designed by Laurie McBarnette

*This book is dedicated to
my lovely wife
"Sam"
with love and gratitude*

CONTENTS

Preface   xi
Introduction   xv

SECTION I—HOW IT BEGINS   1
   Jonathan Bolt—Playwright   5
   Carolyn Rossi Copeland—Producer   17
   George Elmer—General Manager   27
Photo Section—How It Begins   36

SECTION II—CREATING THE PRODUCTION   45
   Terry Burgler—Director   49
   Patricia Zipprodt—Costume Designer   57
   Bert Fink—Press Agent   63
Photo Section—Creating The Production   72

SECTION III—RUNNING THE PERFORMANCE   91
   Marianne Cane—Assistant Stage Manager   95
   Keith Elrod—Master Electrician   103

Joseph Busheme—Wardrobe Master	111
Joseph Patria—Production Carpenter	119
Photo Section—Running The Performance	124
Appendix A—Unions and Organizations	139
Appendix B—Related Reading	143
Glossary	145
Index	151

ACKNOWLEDGMENTS

My thanks go to many people. Most are mentioned in the text. Among those who are not are the staffs at the Kenneth Kaplan Agency and the Dramatists Guild. Adrian Bryan-Brown of Solters, Roskin, and Friedman made it possible for me to interview the *Big River* technicians. Gin Taylor, Elizabeth Fielding, Barli Wakefield, and April Keech provided encouragement and understanding as Hal Williamson, Robert Gunter, Susan Williamson, and Debora Parker read and reread the text as it evolved. Finally, Jeanne Gardner, my editor, has shown patience and understanding as well as taste and professional skill. For that I am very grateful.

PHOTO CREDITS: Bo Wilson of the *Theatre*Virginia staff and Jeremy Johnson of Vanco Stage Lighting were extremely helpful in providing photographs for inclusion in this book. Portraits of Jonathan Bolt and Terry Burgler were provided by the subjects. George Storey took the portraits of Bert Fink and the *Big River* staff.

PREFACE

This is not a "how-to" book. There are a number of fine studies which can give the reader a catalog of specifics about working in the theater. Some of them are listed at the end of this volume. "How to become a director" or "How to become a stagehand" is not the point here.

This is a book of visits with professional theater people as they go about both their daily work and the ongoing work of building a career. Someone once said that theater remains a handicraft industry in an age of mechanization. Like the craftsmen of old, theater people tend to move from job to job with little security and only a vague sense of specialization. It is of interest to note that of the ten people profiled here only two are doing the actual work they trained for in college. The rest have distilled their careers from a wide variety of experiences and opportunities.

If you read carefully you will notice that variations on a certain phrase pop up in almost every one of these stories. "A friend told me about . . ." or "I heard about a job . . ." or "through someone I had worked with." It is an important concept to remember. The theatrical community is a very small one. Considerably fewer than one hundred thousand people, including some fifty thousand actors, make up the entire professional theater family. That includes the people who work in several hundred regional theaters as well as those who work in Broadway and off-Broadway shows in New York. Although a handful of people at the very top of each specialty have reputations strong enough to keep them working on the basis of their names alone, most work comes through networking, or keeping in touch with other people in the business.

In more than twenty years as a theater professional, less than half the work I have done has come "cold"—without a personal contact with the person who has hired me. I was once offered a job playing the leading role in *Fiddler on the Roof* while sitting in an office lounge. A director dropped by just at the moment when his actor had bowed out of a production that was about to go into rehearsal. I knew the director socially, but I had never worked for him. He had never seen me perform but knew of my work through mutual friends. I happened to be in the right place at the right time by accident. Because he trusted what friends had said about me, he felt I could do the job. Without an audition, he offered me a starring role.

The point of this incident is that most theater employment happens by accident and by personal reference. Resume credits may be impressive and training may be at the very best schools and colleges, but personal contact and reputation are far more important. As one of the people in this book said, "Do a good job every time you work because you never know who may be watching."

One other point to watch for: In addition to being talented and well trained, all of the people presented here have been flexible. As opportunities have arisen, they have been willing to take their basic skills and put them to work in a new area or in a different context. If you are thinking about working in the theater, this is an important thing to remember.

Oh, and Good Luck!

Walter Williamson
New York City

INTRODUCTION

You have been ushered to your seat in the theater and handed a program. Around you people are chatting with that special energy that spices a moment like this, and in a few minutes the curtain will rise. You and those around you hope to be swept into an entirely different reality with people you have not known before and at a place you have never been. You hope to laugh, or cry, or both. And you hope to enjoy yourselves or learn something, or both. That's what going to the theater is all about.

In your hands you hold the program. It may be a simple folded sheet or it may be a slick magazine. On its cover is the title of the play and some artwork symbolizing it. There will be a page inside devoted to the actors who make up the cast, and there will be some information about who has produced the play and designed the sets and costumes. There will be information about when the play takes place and how many intermissions there will be. Many people stop reading at this point.

If they would look a little further, they would find a page devoted to another group of people. These include the stage manager, the sound operators, the business managers, and the technicians, who make up what is generally referred to as "the crew." Quite a few patrons never even pause over this page. They have come to see the actors, the sets, and the costumes and to hear the music and see the lighting effects. They care little about who put them there. Their main concern is that they *are* there. The technicians are never seen, so they are seldom thought of. And most people in the theater would agree that this is as it should be. If the technicians have done their work properly, the patrons will never be aware of it. They will only know that the environment of the play looked as it should. The patron in a restaurant should not see the fingerprint of the dish washer on the water glass. The driver of a new car should not see the initials of the assembly line worker carved into the dashboard. The audience member watching the play should never be aware of the work of the technicians who make the magic happen. That's why it seems like magic.

The magic of the theater should be as effortless and as automatic as nature itself, if nature could be compressed into the space of a single setting during the two or three hours of a performance. Lights should appear and disappear at just the right moments to color the background or highlight the performer. Furniture and walls, platforms and curtains should find themselves in the right places as if they got there on their own. Logically, everyone knows that a small army of technicians is operating all these elements. Yet theater depends to a large extent on a concept called "the willing suspension of disbelief." It is like a contract in which the audience agrees to pretend that the play happens by itself so long as the people performing, either on stage or off, do not remind them that it is only a play. Let one piece of scenery bump against another, let one crown fall off an actor's head or one light come up on the right side of the stage when the actor enters from the left and the contract is canceled.

Yet, when the contract is honored—when everything happens as it should and with no apparent effort—we often say that the production looked very "professional." It is an apt description. The professionals are the ones who know how to make the magic happen every time the curtain goes up. That is what they are paid for.

The central event of the theater is the performance—the people we meet and the things they do between the time the curtain goes up and the time it falls. However, the work of making a play happen begins long before scenery is painted or actors' lines are learned. In fact, much of the work of the professional theater takes place in offices like those of any other business.

In theater, the person who initiates a production is called the producer. She or he takes responsibility for the presentation of the play, raises the money necessary to present it, and hires the key people, who then hire staffs to work for them. The producer is the authority figure in the system.

The producer hires a general manager to handle the business aspects of the production. This individual must manage the budget, make up payrolls, file legal and tax forms, and handle other business and legal aspects of the show. Since most general managers handle several productions at once, the general manager will hire a company manager to concentrate on an individual production.

The producer also selects an advertising agency and a separate press agent. The advertising agency is in charge of what the play says about itself through posters, TV spots and newspaper ads. The press agent is in charge of getting other people—critics, feature writers, talk show hosts, entertainment editors of magazines, etc.—to write and talk about the play.

The "creative team" consists of the writer, the director, and the designers. It is the writer who creates the script that excites the producer enough to raise the necessary money and set the project in motion. During most of theater history, writers staged their own plays. If the writer was not available, a principle actor might do the job. But with the rising complexity of technology and the emphasis on psychological reality in writing, the director has emerged as an objective eye. It is the director, in consultation with the producer and the writer, who pulls together the performers and the designers who can realize his or her vision of the play. These choices are carefully made. A set designer, no matter how talented and successful, may not be the right person for a small serious work if his or her main experience is with large flamboyant shows. An actor, no matter how talented or well known, may be bypassed if the director feels that he and the actor cannot work well together.

Perhaps it is because of the pressures of the way plays are produced. Perhaps it is because people have to have very high levels of self-confidence in order to survive in the theater. Perhaps it is overcompensation for the insecurity bred by the constant exposure to rejection. Whatever the cause, people involved in the performing arts tend to have both well-developed egos and a great vulnerability to paranoia. This volatile mixture is made more dangerous by the enormous amounts of money involved in commercial theater. A modern comedy with a single set and only a handful of actors can cost a million dollars to produce on Broadway. A major musical can cost five times that amount. With that kind of pressure, it is little wonder that nerves get frayed and psyches get bruised.

In the noncommercial professional theater the situation is a bit more relaxed. For theaters funded by foundation grants and government and private contributions, there is less pressure to have a hit every time out. But in place of the economic risk there is an expectation of a higher standard of artistic achievement. On Broadway or in regional repertory, theater is a high-tension business.

Theater is many things. It is an art form made up of carefully considered choices linked together to communicate a statement. It is a craft in which technique can often be substituted for inspiration. It is an experiment in which new plays and new ways of doing old plays are constantly being tried. It is also an institution which seeks to preserve a whole body of dramatic literature and tradition. In all of this, professional theater is a business with professional standards of product and practice.

Until recent years many of the unseen theater jobs did not exist. Only in the last quarter century have there been significant numbers of not-for-profit theaters. That designation has opened up a whole range of jobs in arts management. Many theaters now find themselves with historians (called "dramaturges"), outreach directors, education specialists, literary managers, development officers, and a whole range of personnel with titles no one had ever heard of twenty or thirty years ago. New developments in the technologies used in scenery, costumes, lights, and sound have created a demand for workers knowledgeable in the most sophisticated levels of electronics and materials management. Formal business training is required to run a theater front office today, whether the workers know anything about theater or not.

This new level of staffing offers jobs to people who might never have considered working in the performing arts before. It also offers people interested in theater a wider range of entry points.

Long before career choices for women became a burning public issue, a number of women had established themselves in leadership roles in the theater. Although they may not have had it easy, such legendary names as Ellen Drew (grandmother of the famous Barrymore family) and Sarah Bernhardt ran their own production operations in the early 1900s. During the 1950s, Jean Dalrymple, Margaret Webster, Jean Rosenthal, and Lucia Victor, plus those who followed their lead, established successful careers as producers, designers, directors, and stage managers. Today there is no area of show business that considers itself a male-only retreat.

Actors get the glory. They hear the applause and take the bows. Directors get the control. They can move people and things around on the stage as freely as whim or imagination allows. Writers get the satisfaction. They see their ideas become people and places and events with color and drama and life. Producers get the money. If successful and consistent, their returns can be enormous. And the others? What do the stagehands and the box-office clerks and the dressers and the set painters and the prop people and the agents and the lighting operators and the ushers get out of the theater? Most would say that being part of the theater is its own reward. Knowing that you have helped make it happen can be very satisfying. It is not always an easy life. It is not always well paid. Yet most would not trade it for any other way of life. How else could they truly say, "I make magic happen for a living"?

SECTION I
HOW IT BEGINS

The first three stops on our behind-the-scenes tour take in the activities and people involved before a play goes into production. We usually think of the first day of rehearsal as the starting point. But work has been going on for many weeks and months before.

The process begins with the writer. Everything that happens—from raising money to curtain calls—has its origin in the words the writer puts on paper.

Playwrights begin with an idea. Something they have read or seen or thought touches a nerve, and they are inspired to fill out the idea with characters and situations and dialogue. Usually inspiration comes from the writer's own experience. Sometimes the writer is commissioned by a producer or an organization to write a script about a particular subject. A few years ago a well known playwright was paid by a wealthy businessman to write a script about the threat of nuclear war. He wrote a script about a writer who is approached by a wealthy businessman to write a script about the threat of nuclear war. The body of the play had to do with the writer's feelings about being drawn into the politics of national policy. The production, largely funded by the businessman, lasted less than a month on Broadway.

Writers do much of their work in isolation. Alone, they must imagine the characters and situations that will convey their thoughts to an audience. They have at their disposal a wealth of literary and theatrical devices, and it is up to the playwright to choose which ones to use. Will a narrator help move the action along, or can the scenes themselves contain all the information the audience will need? Should the story unfold sequentially, or is it better to jump around in time telling little pieces of the story until the entire plot is known? Should the characters and action be realistic? Or would the idea be better served by symbolic figures speaking poetically obscure language? These are questions the playwright must answer as he or she sits alone trying to shape the original idea into a play.

Often writers will gather actors in a room for an informal reading of the new play. From this kind of reading the playwright gets a sense of how the play sounds, and will often make refinements and changes.

Once the play is shaped to the author's satisfaction, he or she will begin marketing it. This involves sending the script to both commercial producers and to writing competitions which award cash prizes for new scripts. Most plays never go beyond this level. One major national competition screens over twelve hundred scripts each year to find ten to work with in a summer retreat in Connecticut. A commercial producer reports refusing even to read scripts that do not come through literary agents and paying attention to only one in twenty that do. Only a few hundred new scripts are produced each year nationally, and only a few dozen come to Broadway and off-Broadway theaters where significant royalties are paid to the writers.

Producers take the next step toward production. The producer has to be convinced of at least two things before he or she will pay an option fee to the writer, which gives him or her the right to produce the play within a specified length of time. First, the producer has to believe that there is something important about the script that needs to be said in the public forum of the theater. Second, the producer, whether in a commercial setting or in a not-for-profit institution, must feel that the production is worth the investment of time and money required. Once the producer is convinced of these two things, he or she sets up a business structure that will allow the play to move forward toward rehearsals.

The first step is raising money for the project. In commercial theater this money is raised by selling shares of the production to investors. The investors are like stockholders in any corporation. They risk their money in the hope that the production will not only pay back the initial investment, but continue to pay profits once the initial investment has been repaid. In not-for-profit theaters the money comes from grants and contributions as well as from ticket sales. Nonetheless, the producer of a not-for-profit theater must be convinced that a particular play is worth using up a major portion of the yearly budget before that play can go into production.

It is at this point that the general manager comes into the picture. While some producers act as their own general managers, many know nothing about the ins and outs of the business side of producing. That is why they seek the services of a person or firm familiar with the legalities of raising money and the complicated regulations imposed by the various unions involved.

The three people we are about to visit represent these three professions. Yet none of them originally planned to do the work they do today, and all three had only general theater training before arriving by accident at their current occupations.

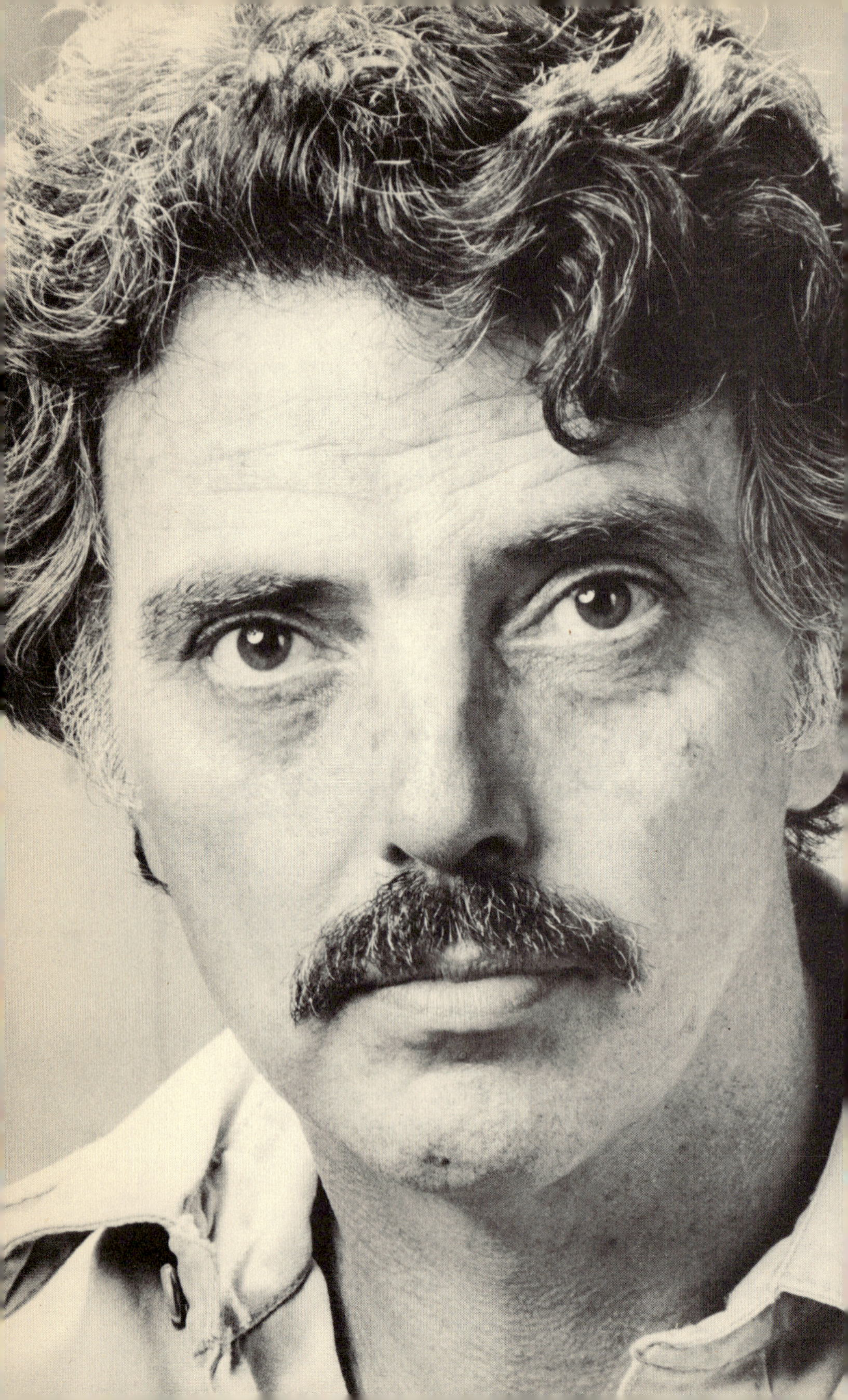

JONATHAN BOLT
PLAYWRIGHT

The guard at the entrance to the White House watched as the taxi pulled to the curb. The man who emerged was tall and handsomely proportioned with clearly defined features and a full shock of dark hair highlighted by patches of silver. There was a natural ease and grace in his movement, and as he approached the guard station, the man in uniform brought himself to a more formal posture. This gentleman might be one of the hundreds of political and industrial figures who carry out business with the President and his staff every day. Or he might be one of the guests invited to celebrate the centennial of the birth of former first lady Eleanor Roosevelt that Mrs. Reagan was sponsoring this morning. The man had the bearing of a diplomat, but when he presented the pass card he had been sent by the Secret Service, he flashed the quick and generous smile of a society patron.

The guard checked the name on the pass against his list. Then he checked the identification the man offered. Returning the papers, the guard looked up and pointed to a doorway. "Certainly, Mr. Bolt. Go right through there. Your party is waiting in the Presidential Library."

The elegantly appointed library had been turned into a dressing room for the day. Actors and costumes were spread out over the rich wood-and-leather furniture, and make-up mirrors were propped on tables designed to support the books and records that presidents and aides use to develop national policy. Jonathan Bolt noted this irony as he chatted with the actors he knew so well. After a while a member of the White House staff invited him upstairs to the East Room where the press had been assembled behind the hundred or so members of Mrs. Roosevelt's family and friends who were there to commemorate the birthday of the nation's most distinguished presidential wife. At one end of the spectacularly decorated chamber, under a vast crystal chandelier, a platform had been erected and the actors played out a musical version of the early life of this painfully plain girl who became one of the most respected figures in the world. Jonathan Bolt had written the script.

One of the charms of living in New York is that you encounter some of the most distinguished and celebrated figures in the world in the most peculiar ways. Jonathan remembered that one day at the beginning of this project he was having some pages reproduced at his local copy shop when the man behind the counter told him that the historian Joseph P. Lash also used that shop for his duplicating. Jonathan had used many of Mr. Lash's books in developing the story of his play because Lash is considered the foremost expert on Mrs. Roosevelt. "I told Mr. Lash that you were doing this musical play about Mrs. Roosevelt," said the copy man. Curious, Jonathan had asked, "What did he say?" "He said he thought it was a lousy idea," said the man flatly. But now Joseph P. Lash and his wife were sitting in the first row near Mrs. Reagan, thoroughly enjoying themselves.

In the receiving line after the performance, Jonathan

was introduced to Nancy Reagan and several of President and Mrs. Roosevelt's children. But the time for congratulations was limited because Jonathan had to catch a plane to Cleveland in order to conduct rehearsals for another show, a new play by Arthur Miller, considered by many to be America's best living playwright. Jonathan was directing the production. He had gone into that project directly from acting in the Broadway production of *Passion*. There isn't much in theater that Jonathan Bolt doesn't do.

Jonathan didn't start out to be a playwright or an actor or a director. He didn't start out in theater at all. Growing up in North Carolina, he displayed a talent for art and worked as a technical illustrator for Bell Telephone Laboratories after graduation from Elon College. Wanting to fortify his art training, he moved on to Virginia Commonwealth University in Richmond, and it was there that he first encountered an alternate use for his gifts. He got involved with set design and was asked to do the designs for a summer theater season in Myrtle Beach, South Carolina. By the time he got back to Richmond in the fall, he had been pressed into acting, and his college major had been changed to Dramatic Arts. But it quickly became clear to Jonathan that it would take longer than he was willing to wait to get a full degree in theater. He decided to pack up and move to New York.

Richmond had given Jonathan several options. He already had a solid professional background in commercial art. He had credentials in set design as well. He had acted some, and he had also written a series of one-act plays that had been highly praised in Richmond. He came to New York with the proof of his various skills packed into a portfolio. It contained examples of his technical illustrations, his set designs, and photographs of his finished scenery. It also contained the only copies of his six one-act plays. One week after he arrived, he accidentally left the entire collection in the back seat of a taxi and never saw it again. It would be almost ten years before Jonathan wrote any more plays.

Acting seemed to be the only thing left that he could prove that he could do. Less than six months later he landed a job in a major Broadway success. Anthony Perkins was playing the leading role in *Look Homeward Angel.* He needed an understudy. Jonathan got the job. Andrew Prine took over the role from Perkins soon thereafter, and Jonathan stayed on to understudy him. Andy was a friend, and when Jonathan told him that his mother and brother were coming to visit, Andy said, "You know, you really ought to play the role when they come to see the show." Kermit Bloomgarden, the producer, was dead set against the idea. But as the time grew closer, Andy said, "You're my understudy. If I just happen to be sick the night your folks are here, you *have* to play the part." The plot was hatched.

When the night arrived, Jonathan got to the theater early, and when the call came from Andy saying he was sick and couldn't go on and that his understudy would have to take over his role for this one performance, Jonathan was ready to get into the costume and perform. He was a great success and his family was thrilled. Not only had they never seen a Broadway show—they had never even seen Jonathan on stage at all. Now he was playing a leading part in a long-running success. When the curtain call came, the entire cast suddenly took two steps back and left him standing in the center of the stage while both audience and actors applauded his outstanding performance.

The next day Jonathan noticed Mr. Bloomgarden backstage and tried to be as casual as possible. Mr. Bloomgarden saw him and said, "I understand there was some excitement here last night." Jonathan, trying to sound as innocent as he could, said, "Yes sir. I'm sorry you didn't get to see it." "Don't worry," said the producer, "I'll see it next Wednesday matinee." Jonathan was surprised and said, "I don't understand." Bloomgarden, fixing him with a stare that told more than his words, said, "Andy Prine has agreed to be sick again."

Jonathan went on to play the role several more times in New York. When the show went on national tour, he was signed to play the role on a regular basis. With that background, he went to Hollywood in 1959 and, for the next five years, worked frequently in television, playing role s in many network series. But his heart was on the stage, and he returned east in the mid-1960s determined to build a career in the theater.

It was during this period of acting and directing that Jonathan met and married Gigi. They had one daughter, Julie, but the marriage did not work out, and they divorced in 1984. It was also during this period that Jonathan took up pen and paper again and developed a screenplay about his early career and his family in North Carolina. Although that piece did not sell right away, it reopened that area of his interest and allowed him to consider writing again. But it would be several more years before his writing would take another leap forward.

In order to provide for his family on a more consistent basis, Jonathan moved them to Cleveland, Ohio, where the Cleveland Playhouse had offered him year-round work as a director. For the next seven years he honed his skills. Toward the end of that time, the urge to write surfaced again, and he produced a lightly satiric play about ancient Egypt called *Eye and the Hands of God*, which was first produced in Cleveland and later at several university theaters. He also dusted off the screenplay about his family and turned it into a stage vehicle called *Threads*.

Returning to New York in the midseventies, Jonathan reestablished his acting career with roles on Broadway, a season of classical repertory off Broadway, and several tours. He also put more energy into his writing, and when *Threads* was accepted for production at the O'Neill Center in 1978, he was delighted. The O'Neill provides ten playwrights every summer with a professional cast and director in order to develop, improve, rewrite, and generally work on their scripts. Like most writing prizes, the value of the O'Neill selection came less from the money it provided and more from the prestige it imparted to Jonathan's career as a writer. On the basis of the O'Neill selection, *Threads* was studied by off Broadway's Circle Repertory Company and, in 1981, Circle Rep mounted a full production of it as part of its regular season.

Having seen *Threads*, the producers of Theatreworks, USA (the largest producer of theater for young audiences in the country) asked Jonathan to submit a proposal for a script about Theodore Roosevelt and his famous Rough Riders. But as Jonathan researched the life of the president who had helped to win the Spanish-American War, built the Panama Canal, and established the National Park system, he became fascinated by the early physical obstacles Roosevelt faced. He had been a sickly child, so to build his stamina, his family had him coached as a boxer. His early sense of rough fair play allowed him to meet and overcome all the challenges he faced in later life. It was that aspect of Roosevelt's life that Jonathan presented to the Theatreworks' producers. To his surprise they liked it and commissioned him to finish the play. It was first produced in 1982 and continued to tour for several more years. *Teddy* was so successful that Theatreworks then commissioned Jonathan to produce a script about Eleanor Roosevelt, Teddy's niece. *First Lady* premiered in 1983 and toured around the country, playing at the New Orleans World's Fair, at several historic sites and, finally, at the White House.

Most recently Jonathan Bolt has scored a great success

with his *To Culebra*, a story about Ferdinand de Lesseps, who built the Suez Canal and his disastrous attempt to build a canal through Panama prior to the American project. A brief outline of how *To Culebra* came into being should give some sense of how a play is written.

Jonathan had first read of de Lesseps while he was working on *Teddy* in 1981. The idea of great men failing in public held his interest, and by the time he had read several books on the de Lesseps affair (which cost France billions and brought down a government), Jonathan knew he wanted to put the story on stage. He continued his research between other projects and made notes and sketches of scenes. In the fall of 1984 he finally sat down and, with three years of research and thinking behind him, turned out a first draft in five weeks of almost nonstop writing. He took the new manuscript to the playwrights' workshop at Circle Repertory, where it was read and commented on by other writers and actors. Taking these comments home, Jonathan revised and refined scenes and bits of dialogue while Circle Rep prepared to produce a formal staged reading of it. In March 1985, nearly four years after work began, *To Culebra* was presented to an audience for the first time by a cast headed by Barnard Hughes.

Thoroughly taken with the piece, agent Robert Friedman agreed to send it to the Humana Festival staged annually by Actors' Theatre of Louisville. The Kentucky festival is arguably the most important forum for new plays in the country. Every year producers and agents from around the world come to Louisville for a showcase of eight new scripts fully staged and rehearsed. The plays open periodically over the course of three weeks. On the final weekend all eight are presented in a repertory marathon that can tax the stamina of both the actors and the audience. But when a play is a hit in Louisville, it can be picked up by companies in Australia, Japan, China, Egypt, Scandinavia, as well as by American companies from Seattle to Broadway. *To Culebra* was a hit in Louisville.

The dust from this explosive success was still settling when Jonathan had to pack up and fly to Sofia, Bulgaria, to direct a play by Tennessee Williams under the sponsorship of the U.S. State Department. Robert Friedman, the agent, would handle inquiries about *To Culebra* for him while he was gone. There was a producer in Alexandria, Egypt, who wanted to do the play immediately. There was another in Copenhagan, as well as interest from several American regional companies and an inquiry from Hollywood. Jonathan had also been approached about a commission to write a new play for Louisville.

"It's funny," Jonathan said during a stopover in New York on his way overseas. "People I've met recently are surprised that I'm going to Bulgaria to direct. They think of me as a writer, and they can't get that out of their heads. Then people who know me as an actor will come up and say they're sorry I've given up acting. The fact is, I haven't given up anything. I still act. I still direct. And now I write."

Bolt is candid about the danger of having his fingers in so many pies. He has never had to take outside jobs to support his theater career because he has been able to respond to a variety of opportunities. At the same time he has suffered from not yet having had an outstanding economic success in any one field. His income has been inconsistent and has ranged from near poverty in some years to moderate comfort in others. Yet he can describe without envy a friend with a Broadway success who takes home nearly $10,000 each week as a royalty based on the standard 10 percent of box-office gross.

When talking about his work as a writer, Jonathan has a clear sense of how and why he works. "All my plays have something to do with my mental state at the time I write them. They come out of some need to express something." He doesn't write daily, but if he's excited about a project, he will sit down and write until he's exhausted. Before he starts he always knows where the play will end, what the last scene will be like and, sometimes, what the last line will be. Then he simply goes back to the beginning and writes toward that end. "The thing I don't like about writing," he says candidly, "is sitting down in a room all by myself and writing." Ironic as that may sound on the surface, he explains that the real fun is seeing something work on a stage.

Bolt works in longhand first, feeling that until something gets into the typewriter it doesn't really count. And he finds the moment when someone else reads a piece for the first time frightening. "You never write what you think you've written. They start asking questions, and you think, 'That's so obvious.' But it's not. So you take that criticism and go home and curse and say, 'I never should have started this in the first place,' and you sleep on it and finally it sinks in and you go on and fix what has to be fixed."

Jonathan is aware of the standard advice to young writers to "write what you know." But he has a warning about autobiographical work on the stage: "They never get it right," he says. "If you're writing about real people you know, the actors can never really be the people you see when you write." His own experience with *Threads* taught him that. The character of the mother was written with love and sympathy. But the director on one production had not had a good experience with his own mother and guided the actress playing the role toward villainy. As author, Bolt had to work with both the director and the performer to show them the positive interpretation of what, in black and white, could have gone either way.

From his history of work in every phase of theater, Jonathan Bolt has poured experience and talent into his writing.

Yet, he continues to resist being tied down to any one form of expression. He smiles an actor's smile when he says, "The writing isn't as interesting to me as seeing something work on the stage. As a theater person, that's what's really important."

Jonathan Bolt works as much as an actor as he does as a writer. His acting agent uses the picture on page 4 to submit Jonathan for jobs. (Photo courtesy of J. Bolt.)

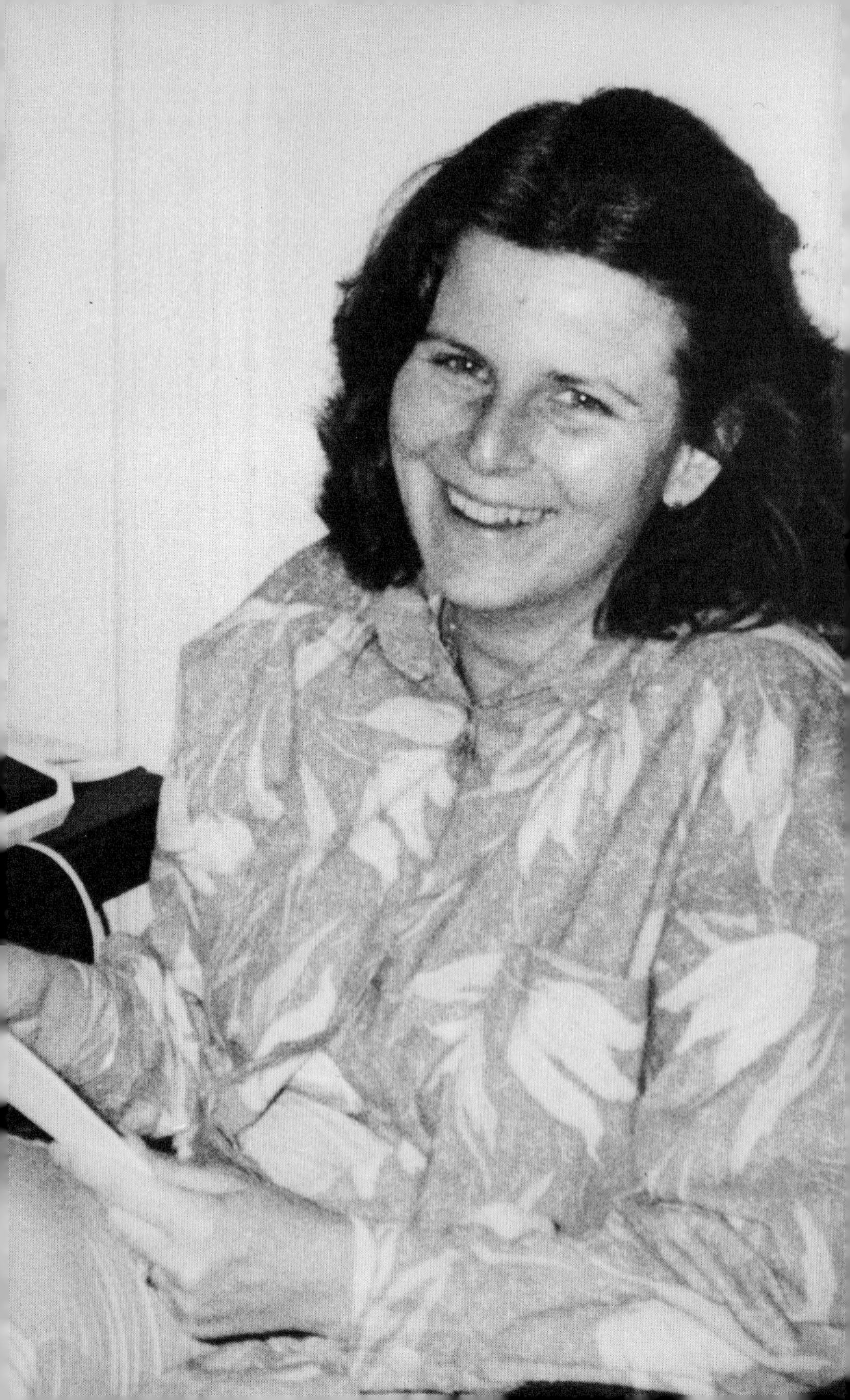

CAROLYN ROSSI COPELAND

PRODUCER
THE LAMB'S THEATRE

One of the people at the table was a star. He had played leading roles on television, in films and on Broadway. He was nominated for a Tony award a year or so before, and his face was instantly recognizable. The second person at the table was the writer whose play the star was interested in doing. The third person was Carolyn Rossi Copeland, who was in a position to make it all happen. Carolyn is the producer of the Lamb's Theatre, and it was there that the meeting was taking place.

Suddenly, the fourth person at the table started to make noise, and Carolyn turned to the two men. "I hope you don't mind?" she said. As the men nodded, Carolyn picked up her three-week-old daughter, Margaret, and discreetly began to nurse her while she continued to lead the discussion of the forthcoming production. When you're the boss, you do things your own way.

Carolyn Rossi Copeland does things her own way. As producer of the Lamb's Theatre Company, she operates two theaters in a landmark building originally designed as a private club for members of the theatrical profession back when gentlemen's clubs farther uptown would not allow "theatricals" as members. Situated just off Times Square, the building was purchased from the Lambs Club by the Manhattan Church of the Nazarene in the early 1970s.

It was because of the church that Carolyn first became a professional producer. But that comes later.

First let's go to Washington, D.C., and the offices of Congressman Peter Rodino. It is 1973, and Rodino has become one of the best-known faces in America. As chairman of the House Judiciary Committee, Rodino ran the nationally televised hearings that voted the historic articles of impeachment against Richard Nixon. In Washington, public exposure is power. Peter Rodino is powerful.

Working for Rodino as a special assistant in charge of managing events, dinners, fund-raising parties, press conferences, etc., is young Carolyn Rossi, recent graduate of Tulane University with a degree in Political Science and an international background that includes living in New York, Rome, and the U.S. Virgin Islands.

When the congressman's secretary calls Carolyn into Rodino's office, there doesn't seem to be anything out of the ordinary going on. The congressman is behind his desk apparently looking at a magazine. But as soon as the door is closed his reedy voice lifts in a way that shocks the young assistant. "What is the meaning of this?" he demands. "What, sir?" is the only response the young assistant can make. Rodino turns the magazine around and pushes it toward the tense young woman. "I thought I was supposed to be the one getting press coverage, not you!" There, on the pages of a periodical devoted to life in the Washington area, is a picture of Carolyn and an article about how she has choreographed a musical-theater piece for a prominent Washington club. At that same moment, Carolyn realizes that the congressman is chuckling to himself. She is relieved that the outrage is a joke, and, as Rodino asks questions, she explains that dance and theater have always been a part of her life. She first began ballet classes in Rome when she was eight. She continued to study when she could after her family moved back to St. Thomas in the Virgin Islands. At Hollins College in Virginia, and later at Tulane, she held theater as her major free-time activity. "But," she says, "I knew my Italian/American father would not pay for a theatrical education, so I majored in something more practical: Political Science." Rodino nods and smiles. The two share the same pride in their Italian heritage and understand the authority figure of the Italian father—one as its subject, one as its object.

The thin but melodious voice of the congressman mellows slightly as he asks, "Is this what you really want to do?" Carolyn hesitates a moment, sensing that something important is about to be said. "Yes," she says with both fear and hope mingled with the courage required to make such a statement. The powerful politician fixes her with his eyes for what seems like a long time. When he speaks it is heartfelt and fatherly and friendly and a bit melancholy. "Then I think you ought to go do it."

Carolyn is stunned, and the look on her face prompts the older man to remove a layer of the public posture of passionless objectivity that adds so much weight and substance to his leadership. "I'm a frustrated opera singer," says Peter Rodino. "I wanted to sing the great tenor roles. But I had to do the 'practical' thing. So I became a lawyer and a politician. But I always wondered where I might have been now if I hadn't been so practical."

And so, Carolyn Rossi left Washington on Rodino's promise that if theater didn't work out for her, she could come back to work for him. She went on tour with a company doing musicals for dinner theaters and saw from the inside how professional productions were put together. Producing had always seemed an exotic and complicated process to Carolyn. But watching the company operate, she couldn't help thinking, "I could do that."

She got her chance in a most unexpected way. She relocated to New York and remained busy choreographing musicals for small theater groups around the city. She taught some and directed some and developed enough of a resume and a reputation to be invited to do a play for the Church of the Nazarene, which had just taken over the Lambs Club. The building contained an empty 370-seat theater. She directed two productions for them, *Godspell* and *You're a Good Man, Charlie Brown*. Then she decided to take a break and go home to visit her family in St. Thomas.

Like most tourist sites, St. Thomas seems like an isolated world unto itself. Visitors see the lush green of the tropical gardens, the quaint red roofs of the buildings, the busy commerce of the duty-free port, and the languid stretches of beach that surround the island. But there is another St. Thomas made up of permanent residents and island natives. There are grocery stores and garages and private homes and pet shops as in any community. There is also a fine college on a spacious campus just west of the airport. Since most of the tourist hotels and attractions are east of the airport, few tourists get to see this flower-covered asset. That is, unless they come to see a performance at the Reichold Center for the Performing Arts, an asset within the asset. The theater has an enclosed stage, but the audience sits outside, charmed one moment by the scent of tropical flowers in the surrounding gardens, the next moment by the warm breeze that gently lifts off Brewer's Bay just across the road.

When Carolyn came home to St. Thomas for that visit in 1977, she was going through a period of frustration and self-doubt. She had worked a lot, and the work had been good. But she was beginning to wonder if her work as a performer or as a choreographer would ever be great. She loved theater. She loved to dance and direct. She wanted the professional stage she respected to be peopled by the very best, not just people who were good. And too, she had a lot of experience but very little formal training in theater. She questioned whether she could give the quality she expected to see in others.

At the same time she was going through some profound spiritual questioning. Her traditional Roman Catholic observance was being challenged by the more spontaneous and emotional worship she witnessed when she occasionally attended services with the Nazarenes who had brought her into the Lamb's family. Her Christian commitment was never in question. The form that commitment would take had some very gray areas. The same was true of her theater anxiety. She knew she was talented and devoted to using that talent. She was simply not sure how that talent and devotion could best serve the theater she loved.

Then her parents suggested she drive out to see the new Reichold Center which had been built during her time away from the island. She put it off until the last day of her visit. She wasn't sure seeing a beautiful new stage would do anything to clarify the confusion she was feeling. But when she pulled off the main road into the vibrant green canyon that rises from the blue Caribbean Sea, she was awestruck by the sheer beauty of the place. The theater nestled into the mountains that rose around it, and the stage stretched out welcoming arms around the open-air seats. Carolyn was impressed.

She arranged to meet Maggie Klekas, the executive director of the center, and when the two women talked the rapport was instant. Maggie, tall, slender, and angular, with blond hair and a nervous energy that covers a solidly accurate mind, sat beside small dark-haired Carolyn, whose calm exterior tends to hide the excitement and determined power within. Maggie was explaining how delays in the opening of the theater itself had made it difficult to schedule a full season of performing events. She was having trouble finding companies that could fill out her mandate to provide all kinds of performances for the college and for the people of the island.

Suddenly Carolyn heard herself saying that she could bring in the two shows she had just directed at the Lambs in New York. The performers, mostly young and out of work, would likely jump at the chance to work professionally in this tropical paradise for a few weeks. The sets were simple and could travel fairly easily. Maggie was getting excited. Carolyn could not believe herself as she rattled on about what she could and could not provide. Then Maggie was saying, "Get me a budget and a press kit, and I think we're in business."

Carolyn Rossi was a producer. Just like that. She called New York and told one of her associates to round up the cast. Then she hopped a plane north and started producing. There were contracts to make with the publishers of the scripts. There was a production budget to prepare. There were dozens of questions about transporting actors and costumes and sets and props. There were press releases to write and photographs to be taken so that Maggie in St. Thomas could get started with the promotion. Everyone pitched in. Take this contract over to the airline office. Pick up photographs from the overnight copy store. Check the costumes to make sure everything is still there. The list of details seemed endless. Carolyn found herself giving orders and delegating responsibility. She couldn't keep up with the details herself. But she found that her enthusiasm and excitement were infecting the dozen or so people who were working with her. She was helping them to accomplish an almost impossible task with joy and dedication. Carolyn knew she was faking it, but she was also learning as she went along.

She also found that her frustration and doubt were wiped away by the pace she was forced to maintain in order to see this project through. She didn't have time to wonder about her talent or her commitment—she was too busy living them out.

When the St. Thomas project was over and had proven successful, the church asked Carolyn to stay on and develop a theater program in the building. They put her on the church staff and helped her raise funds for a series of children's theater pieces that also were successful. But it was clear that more ambitious work needed to be found. During the next several years Carolyn tried a variety of projects and formats. Clearly there was potential. Clearly there was interest. Clearly there was a theater facility available in the heart of Times Square that could house a style of theater both competitive in the mainstream marketplace and consistent with the uplifting and positive viewpoint shared in both Carolyn's personal beliefs and the mandate of the church which was home to the project. The question was the same one Carolyn had wrestled with before: How could the resources be best used?

Carolyn did not want to run a "Christian" theater company. The cynical world of New York theater could too easily dismiss such an effort and label it unimportant because of its religious influence. Whatever work the company did would have to be competitive with the best available theater in the major Broadway houses. That meant several things. First, the theater would have to have a facelift. Second, and most important, the quality of work offered must be watched constantly to make sure the best artistic standards were maintained. Finally, the work must be presented with neither labels nor apologies. If audiences began to notice that productions at the Lamb's Theatre consistently represented respect for family values, spiritual strength and uplifting themes, so much the better. But first the work must be worthy of being seen by anyone from any background on the basis of its artistic quality alone.

The theater was renovated in time to open the 1981 season with *Cotton Patch Gospel*, a dynamic musical interpretation that set St. Mark in rural Georgia and spiced the brew with songs by Harry Chapin. The production was a great success and paved the way for a number of outstanding productions, including *Painting Churches*, *Breakfast with Les and Bess*, and the recent revival of *Dames at Sea*. Most of these shows were organized by outside producers and booked into the Lamb's with coproduction cooperation from Carolyn and her core staff of four.

By renovating the landmark theater at the Lamb's and by booking quality productions that carried themes consistent with Carolyn's personal perspective and that of the church, Carolyn had created a new Broadway theater in which small productions of quality scripts could have a graceful home. But in the process Carolyn had become more a landlord than a producer, and it was clear that her creative work was not over.

By now Carolyn had married Jamie Copeland, an outstanding young architect. It was Jamie who redesigned what had been a members' dining room in the old club house into an intimate theater space now called the Lamb's Downstairs. Now Carolyn could manage the main theater upstairs and produce her own shows in the smaller downstairs theater. In the four years of its operation, the downstairs theater, like its big brother upstairs, has been home to an array of fine shows. Carolyn Rossi Copeland has managed to create two thriving professional theater operations in a space that only a few years ago was an empty antiquated auditorium.

Carolyn is very clear in her understanding of her function. "The most important thing I do is pick the scripts. If they are not right, then nothing that follows is right." At the same time she is very clear about her limitations. "My gift," she says, "is in motivating people, getting them organized. I'm not good at the details. We have people who are good at follow-through. My gift is in getting the ball rolling." She is also critical of producers who leave too much to others. "I'm here every night saying the coffee tastes rotten, the ushers aren't dressed properly, the lobby needs cleaning. It's important for a producer to pay attention to what's going on—and not just on the stage." Far from being seen as a tyrant, though, Carolyn's critical observations are respected by the staff she has assembled. They know that because of her watchful eye, the Lamb's Theater has developed a reputation for being well run and honest in a field that is not known for being either businesslike or consistently ethical.

That loyalty gives Carolyn the flexibility to do things her way. "Where else could I keep my baby next to my desk and nurse her whenever I need to? Theater is a family. That's what I like about it." She also likes the fact that she can involve herself in many different aspects of the operation. She picks the plays, negotiates contracts with artists, watches over the office, checks the appearance of the facility and the staff. All those bits and pieces go into the job of producing.

When asked to describe herself, Carolyn has a list of similarly diverse elements. "I'm a child of God, who is still a child and able to make mistakes. I'm a wife and a mother. I'm a producer. I'm a kid who says, 'Gee, isn't this fun' when we're here painting scenery at two in the morning." Clearly, in both her life and in her work, Carolyn Rossi Copeland has put all the bits and pieces together and used them well. Very well, indeed.

In the photo on page 16 Carolyn Rossi Copeland checks out the box office. She believes a producer must be involved with every aspect of the presentation.

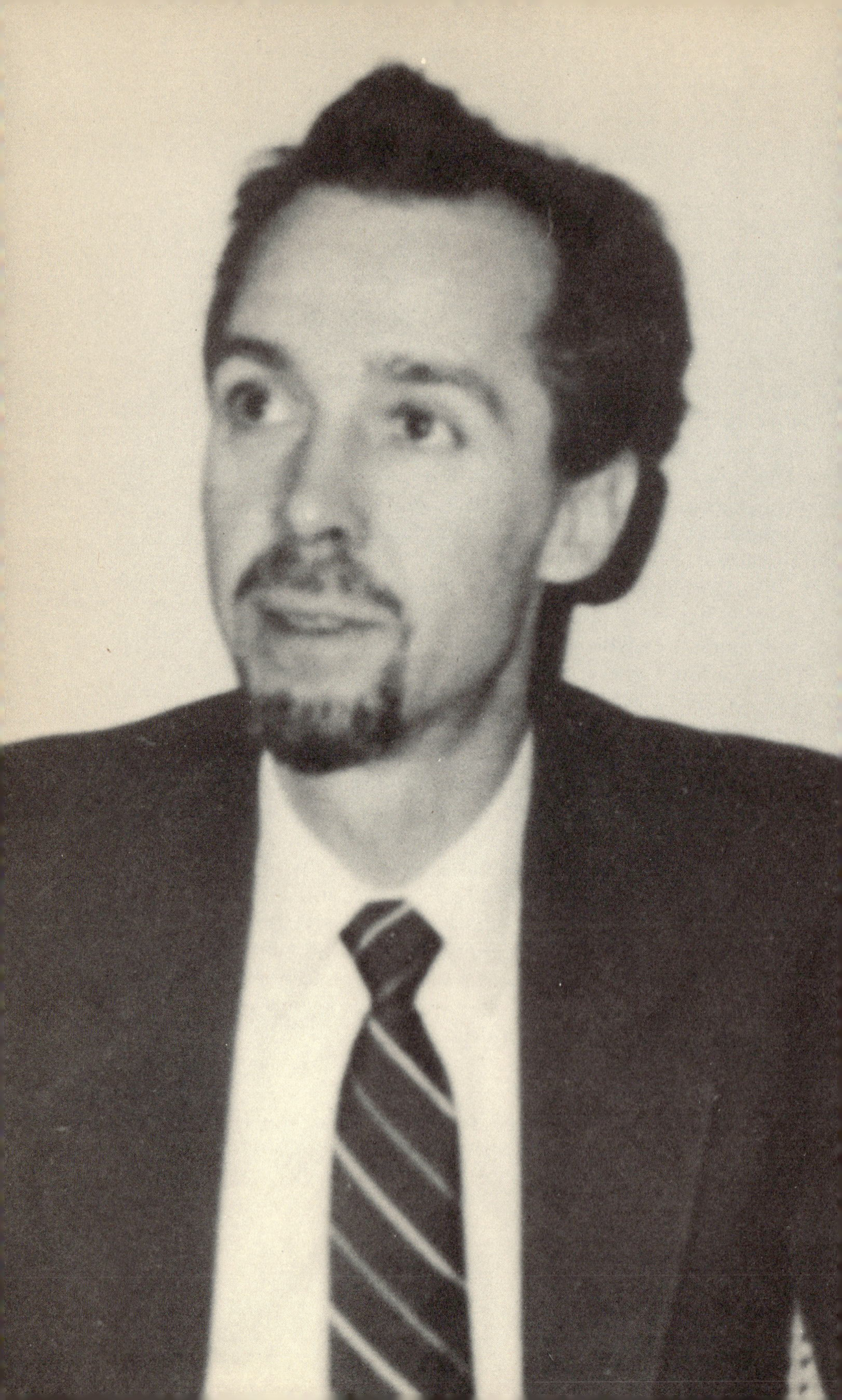

GEORGE ELMER
GENERAL MANAGER
DOROTHY OLIM ASSOCIATES, INC.

It wasn't George's idea. He had no real interest in theater. Oh, he had been to a few plays. But there were several other ways a sailor could spend his last night in London before returning to the states. Going to see *My Fair Lady* was not George's idea. But the people he was with wanted to go. So he went. And his life was never the same again.

Drury Lane is known to more people as the home of the Muffin Man in the children's rhyme than as the home of one of London's oldest and most prestigious theaters. It is a vast hall with balconies and boxes, heavy velour drapings and gilded ornaments and fixtures in the old-fashioned style. Sitting in any one of over a thousand plush seats, you can look up to see if anyone in the Queen's family is in the royal box. If anyone royal was there on that night in 1962, George does not remember. What captured his memory then and held it ever since was the magical musical play on the stage. Julie Andrews was playing Eliza Doolittle, fresh from her triumphant New York performance that made her into a star. Edward Mulhare had replaced Rex Harrison for the London engagement, but the rest of the cast was the same as in the Broadway production that had broken every popularity record ever kept.

George had already made plans. He had joined the navy fresh out of high school. An exceptional student in math and science, he was prepared to attend MIT as soon as his navy hitch was up. He would spend the rest of his life in the abstract world of numbers. Or so he thought until he saw *My Fair Lady*. "Magic is the only word for it," says George today. "It's a perfect piece of theater."

George was so stirred by that production that something in him insisted on being part of the world that made things like that happen. On leaving the Navy he canceled his MIT plans and enrolled in the theater program at Virginia Commonwealth University. The program was intensive and gave him an opportunity to work in every phase of production from building scenery to acting, from sewing costumes to directing. He plunged into the heavy production schedule, and when not assigned to a show he would often volunteer to work on it in his minimal free time. People who knew him then say he carried a clipboard as if it were an outgrowth of his hand, and that he absorbed and cataloged details with the efficiency of a human theatrical encyclopedia.

One day Raymond Hodges, then head of the VCU drama department, called George into his office. "George," said the older gentleman, "We spend a lot of time trying to keep people from going into theater. It's just too hard a profession for most of the people who come through here as students. But you. . . ." Mr. Hodges paused. "George, you belong in the professional theater." That meeting with Ray Hodges is just one of many details that have stayed with George over the years—one of many, many details that have shaped an individual and personal attitude toward the work he now does every day.

It is the details that make the difference between something merely good and something special—something that could truly be called "professional quality." George saw this early on and knew instinctively that if the individual pieces were properly attended to, then the final product would fit together smoothly, beautifully, and professionally. In a way, George saw it like math; if you balance the individual parts of the equation, the formula works.

Today George Elmer heads one of the half dozen or so top management firms in New York, Dorothy Olim Associates, which has handled the business affairs of an impressive list of Broadway and off-Broadway productions including *The Curse of the Aching Heart* with Faye Dunaway, *Solomon's Child* with Anthony Zerbe, and *Maybe I'm Doing It Wrong* with Randy Newman. As general manager for a production, George's work is filled with details. "I spend 60 to 70 percent of my life reading," he says. "There are contracts which can run to sixty pages, there are new scripts to be considered, there are union rules to read and interpret, there are letters and lists and bills and financial statements. Beyond that I try to see as much theater as possible. That means I end up at home only two or three nights a week."

George, who has been at Dorothy Olim for five years, has become one of the most well respected members of the small management fraternity. But he has not always been as well known or as relatively secure as he is today. In the nearly twenty years that he has worked professionally, there have been some lovely "ups." But there have been at least as many "downs."

George left college after his junior year. "I wasn't unhappy. I just didn't feel I would need the degree itself, and I thought I could learn more by actually going out and getting to work." He first considered New York, but was offered an internship with the Director's Guild of

America, learning film and television direction. It meant a move to the West Coast, where he very quickly realized that he had no love for Hollywood. "By the end of a year I had acted in two commercials and worked as assistant director on a couple of films. My tax return showed that I had made just over $84,000. But after agents' commissions, managers' fees, taxes, and working expenses like photographs, clothes, and transportation around the world's largest parking lot, I actually saw about $22,000." George decided to leave California before he started hating it. On the way to the airport, his car was rear-ended by a loaded gravel truck. For the next several months George hurt and healed and looked forward to going back east, back to the theater he loved and felt at home in whether he was making money or not. California had not proved to be a hospitable host. Little did he know that California had not finished being inhospitable to him.

Returning east, George became stage manager for a Philadelphia-based dance company. He fell in love with one of the dancers and they planned to marry. But her father insisted George go back to Richmond and finish his degree. For the sake of peace in the family, George grudgingly agreed.

With his degree in one hand and Rosanne on the other, George finally headed north and settled in New York. He was lucky. Through a friend he heard that *Jacques Brel Is Alive and Well and Living in Paris* needed a stage manager. For the next five years George was involved with both the New York and touring productions of the long-running show.

Then came the opportunity for George to stage-manage a Los Angeles production of *Jacques Brel*. He had a new son, Jason, and George thought California might give his family a more open environment than New York could offer. The Elmers packed up their belongings and crossed the country. There was talk of a great boom in live theater in California. They would be there as it began.

For a while, everything went well. The show was a great success, and the immediate future looked rosy. Then the production changed producers and theaters. One day George and the company arrived at the theater, but the producer did not. As they waited and waited, George began to get a sinking feeling. He had heard stories about this kind of thing, but he never thought it would happen to him. Sure enough, the new producer had disappeared with all the company money and suddenly George was stranded in California with a wife, a six-month-old son, and no job. The California theater boom was as phony as a Hollywood special effect. With no legitimate-theater market for his skills, George took the most distasteful job of his entire career. In order to feed his family, he hired on to operate the lights and play the music tapes for the strippers in a topless bar. Until he could find something better, he would just have to survive.

As quickly as he could, George took a different job selling sound equipment. The money was good, "but not *that* good." He and Rosanne were meeting expenses but not getting very far ahead. "I had to say, 'Wait a minute. What is it I'm trying to do here? What is it I'm trying to accomplish?'" Seeing situations clearly in all their details was always a strong skill, and as George looked at his situation, he realized that California was not the place for him or his family. They belonged back in the theater. And the theater was headquartered in New York. It took several more months of temporary jobs, but finally, due to clear thinking, attention to detail, and plain old hustle, George and Rosanne finally had enough money saved to rent a truck and head back to New York, back to the theater, back home.

As soon as they were back in the city, George put his

hustle to work and called everyone he knew. Within a day after their return, he found work as house manager of the Astor Place Theatre, supervising the ushers, running the lobby area and generally taking care of the audience. This work was somewhat new for George. Most of his experience had been behind the curtain—performing, directing, and stage-managing. Now he wore a tie and met and greeted the public. He also began to catalog the differences between the performing aspects of theater and the management aspects.

When he had been in Hollywood George had often heard the phrase "the suits are here." It was said with disdain by cast and crew. It meant that some people from the front office had come on the set. You could always tell who they were. They wore business suits. Casts and crews, whether in films or on the stage, develop a family feeling. The shared experience of creative work draws people together and contributes to what is called an "ensemble" feeling. When outsiders arrive, particularly those who have management authority over the group, their presence is felt as an intrusion. It is the same feeling students get when a teacher or principal enters an all-student conversation. It may be an entirely friendly visit. But the presence is an alien one and not completely welcome. Although the phrase is not used as frequently in New York as it is in California, George realized that he had become a "suit." And he was not uncomfortable in his new role.

When the opportunity came to manage the office of a busy theatrical press agent, George slipped into yet another facet of front-office work. For the next five years he helped handle press releases, opening-night parties, invitations to critics and newspaper writers for a variety of Broadway shows, including three productions starring Katherine Hepburn, *Romantic Comedy*, magician David Copperfield, and both the twentieth- and twenty-fifth-anniversary revivals of *My Fair Lady* starring Rex Harrison.

By now George had acted, directed, stage-managed, booked touring productions for the civic theater in Philadelphia, run the front of the house at the Astor Place, and handled promotion in a press agent's office. Each job had its own language and its own unique character. George had learned them all. He could discuss acting with actors and directing with directors. He could estimate the number of people in an audience just by looking, and he could estimate the cost of printing and mailing a press release just by checking the number of people it was going to. The details of union regulations and costs, schedules and travel requirements for tours, weekly costs for rented equipment, and weekly box-office receipts were all becoming part of George's catalog. Each new experience could be distilled into a series of dos and don'ts, facts and figures, regulations and priorities. Experience became knowledge, and each new piece of knowledge got filed away in George's mental catalog. As the catalog expanded, so did George's value as a theater-management professional. When a friend told him about the opening at the Dorothy Olim office for a company manager, handling the day-to-day business affairs of an off-Broadway production, George was ready for the challenge.

As a company manager, George found himself filing contracts with union offices and keeping statistical records about attendance and box-office receipts. He paid bills and supervised payrolls. He computed overtime payments for extra performances and approved orders for backstage supplies. George proved himself more than competent in his new position. When the general manager's chair at Dorothy Olim became empty, George was asked to fill it.

As general manager for a production, George is involved directly with the producer in drawing up production budgets and analyzing financial and artistic decisions. George helps negotiate contracts with performers and designers and gives advice on advertising campaigns and selections of theaters. A general manager can, in fact, do almost everything a producer can do. Almost—but not quite.

"There are three things a producer cannot delegate," says George. "A producer must pick the product. The producer is the only person who can decide that a play is going to be done. Then a producer must finance the production, draw in the investors. Finally, a producer must absorb the losses or pocket the profits. Everything else can be delegated. Those three jobs cannot be delegated." When asked about the nature of his work, George explains that often first-time producers know nothing about mounting productions. They have found a script that they feel must be seen. It becomes the general manager's job, then, to help the producer get the best possible production for the least amount of money.

"Why do producers produce? The obvious answer is 'to make money.' And in a commercial theater that is as it should be. But the reality," George says, "is that people produce plays for the same reason actors become actors: They have to. They don't have a choice in life. There's an internal mechanism driving them to produce a play they care deeply about."

A general manager helps the producer make choices and decisions. If the producer wants to handle everything on his own, then the general manager will simply follow a prepared budget and pay the bills. If, on the other hand, the producer wants a lot of help, the general manager is there with skills for everything except picking the project, financing it, and attending to the financial bottom-line profit or loss. The general manager bases the management fee on how much or how little of the other work he participates in.

The Dorothy Olim office accepts only some of the work that is offered to them. "Life's too short to work on plays you don't enjoy with people you don't respect," says

George. For that reason they maintain veto power over the selection of stage managers and house staff, who are their direct contact with the business aspects of each show. They also read a script very carefully before committing their services to it so they can feel that they and the producer see the same things to admire in it. "I am very proud to say," George says, "that I have never lost that youthful idealism most people think you're supposed to lose like baby fat."

That idealism extends to his family as well. Rosanne taught dance with the distinguished Elliot Feld Company until recently. But she wanted to be a full-time mom to Jason, now thirteen, and his brother Luke, now seven. They have a large comfortable apartment in the North Bronx and George commutes by subway. George anticipates producing on his own eventually, and hopes for other chances to direct. For the moment, however, he enjoys putting the details together for other producers, and he gets a great deal of satisfaction from maintaining standards of quality in both his life and his work.

Yet George is realistic about what he does. "There are no guarantees in life," he says thoughtfully. "There are good times and bad times. There are successful productions and those that are not. If one is in the 'business of show,' it is not by free choice, it is by manic compulsion. If you have to be here, you will be here." He pauses only briefly before underlining the simplicity and clarity of his view. "If you don't *have* to be here, get an MBA and enjoy the corporate life."

In the photo on page 26, George Elmer stands by the box office of one of his shows. Although the company manager does the day-to-day work, George looks in frequently. (Photo by George Storey)

36 BEHIND THE SCENES

The audience has gone home.

The stage is empty.

Alone, the writer must use history, imagination, and centuries of theatrical tradition to develop a new play to fill the empty stage. (Writer Jonathan Bolt works on script changes for his play To Culebra.)

When it is finished, the script must be typed up in proper professional form. (A page from the author's play Porter's Brandy. *Notice that actor's directions are indented to one space while general directions are indented to another. Also note the page number. This is actually page 46 of the text, but it is numbered as the first page of Act II.)*

ACT II

Scene 1

    (WILLIAM appears alone in his light)
         WILLIAM
The rage comes from being alone. The rage comes from seeing everyhing that's wrong and feeling powerless to change it--make it right. The rage comes from being less and wanting more. The rage comes from being taught to respect the pattern and then seeing that the pattern was not designed by a merciful God--but by a white devil. The rage comes--and it does not go away.

    (WILLIAM retires as the single light
    fades into the room light)

        It is evening of the following day.
        The only significant change is the
        addition of a large green glass
        demijohn on the left table in which
        have been arranged a few lillies.

    (DORA is lighting candles around the room
    There seems to be no other light source.
    SHE stops at a burst of laughter from off
    left and smiles in satisfaction)

         MISS MARGARET
    (Enters and goes immediately to the light switch
    near the front hall
Still out?

         DORA
Yessum. Thank the Lord I got that coffee perked 'fore the power went. How's it going in there?

         MISS MARGARET
Fine. How's Yolanda doing?

         DORA
She spooked a little when everything went off, but I got her some candles back there and she fine now.

         MISS MARGARET
Dora, I have to say this meal has been one of your finest hours.

         DORA
It is good, ain't it.

         MISS MARGARET
Now onward to the brandy. We'll serve that in here, then take the gentlemen out to the porch.

television, touring performances, stock performances, Broadway performances, off-Broadway performances, original cast albums, tapes, cassettes and records made therefrom and video cassettes or discs, photographic reproductions of the actor presenting the Play whether as posters or as books.

If the Producer has presented an official opening of the play but less than thirty (30) consecutive paid public performances of the play in New York City as herein provided he shall receive five (5%) percent of performer's receipts from all subsequent uses.

If the Producer has presented thirty (30) or more consecutive paid public performances of the Play he shall receive ten (10%) percent of the Performer's receipts from all subsequent uses.

For the purposes of computing the number of paid public performances , provided the Play officially opens in New York City the computation of the foregoing shall commence with the first paid public performance.

In the event the play does not have an official opening in New York City, only the first fifteen paid public performances shall apply in the computation of the foregoing, except that Actor requests Producer not to officially open and Producer grants such request, in which case all paid public performances shall apply to the foregoing computation.

When the script is ready, it is submitted to various producers who might be interested in raising the money necessary and arranging a production. (Carolyn Rossi Copeland, producer of the Lambs' Theater, works in a cozy office on the third floor of the theater.)

Once a producer has shown interest a legal document must be drawn up giving the producer the "option" to produce the work. This document becomes the basis for setting up the business side of a production. The language of these documents is highly technical and has little to do with the artistic content of the planned production. (This is a page from an option agreement for a production of a one-man-show version of The Gospel According To Saint Luke.)

Theater, like any other business, takes advantage of the latest business technology. (Carolyn Rossi Copeland and an assistant at The Lambs' Theater keep records on a computer.)

Although tickets may be ordered by mail or by telephone, there must still be a box office at the theater to keep track of the actual tickets sold for any given performance. (Carolyn Rossi Copeland at the Lambs' box office.)

Institutional companies like the Lambs' have their own theaters and most are supported by contributions and grants as much as from ticket sales. Commercial producers, on the other hand, must face the competition that is Broadway. This block, Forty-fifth Street between Seventh and Eighth Avenues, is the heart of Broadway, with eight theaters (The Minskoff, The Booth, The Plymouth, The Royale, The Golden, The Imperial, The Music Box and The Marquis) opening onto a single street. Each is rented to the current production for a percentage of ticket receipts.

Commercial theater is always a gamble. This production closed after only a few performances with a loss to investors of several million dollars.

(Photo Credits: 1, 2, courtesy of TheatreVirginia; 3–10 from the author's collection.)

SECTION II
CREATING THE PRODUCTION

Out of the darkness a voice suddenly says, "Thank you. I'll let you know." The person on the stage who hears that curt dismissal might be an actor auditioning for a role in the play. Or a costume designer who might be showing a new version of a costume that didn't work the first time around. Or a prop designer who is offering a choice between two different chairs he has found. The person who makes the choices about what goes on the stage and what does not—the person behind the voice—is the director. The director takes the play that the writer has created and, filtering it through his or her own artistic vision, brings the play to life on the stage.

The process starts with the script. The director and the writer may talk for weeks about scenes and characters. They may think about making changes in the dialogue. They may decide to alter the time or place of a scene. They come to know the script as if it were a living person.

Next, the director, with the help of the producer, hires designers who can turn the director's ideas into physical realities. Scenery and costumes are more than just locations and clothing. With choices of color and line, style and texture, a designer can convey a mood or a feeling that can help or hurt a scene. A simple example can be drawn from the Broadway production of *A Chorus Line*. The characters are all in rehearsal clothes—jeans, T-shirts, leotards, and tights. Although there is no "lead" in the show, one of the dancers gets singled out for a solo number. She wears a dark red jersey skirt. When she stands in the line with the other characters, the costume blends into the group and the actress doesn't seem any more special than the others. Yet, when she does her solo number the skirt gives her a kind of regal grace that enhances both her character and the dance she performs. If the skirt were a brighter shade, she would stand out from the crowd before she is supposed to. If it were any darker, the dance would not look quite so special. Finding just the right shade of red was a major design decision. Multiply that choice by the hundreds of such choices that must go into a production that may have several sets and dozens of costumes, and you begin to see the value of good designers.

Directors and designers work together with sketches and examples of colors, photographs of buildings, and drawings of furniture to achieve just the right look for a production. Once the director and the designers understand each other, the designers go off to work in their studios while the director goes to work actually directing the actors who will perform the play.

Directors select actors through an audition process whereby hundreds of actors may be seen and talked to before a few are actually allowed to read from the script for each role. Qualities of personality and physical presence that have nothing to do with a performer's acting talent come into play. If a director is casting a family, and both parents are short, the director may pass up a very good actor for the role of their son simply because the actor happens to be too tall.

Once a cast has been selected and contracted, rehearsals begin. During these sessions, which can last from a week in summer stock to six or eight weeks for a Broadway show, movement and characterization are explored. The director may act as a puppeteer, telling every actor exactly where to go and what to do. Or the director may work in a freer style, allowing the actors to grow into their roles slowly and spontaneously. Good directors know that while they set the pattern, it is ultimately the actors who will have to face the audience. For that reason good directors make sure their performers are comfortable with the way scenes are to be played.

While all this work is going on in scenic and costume shops and in rehearsal studios, advertising agencies and press agents are busy sending out information and photographs and trying to stimulate a theater audience so that when the actors and the scenery and the costumes all come together on the stage, there will be someone there to watch them.

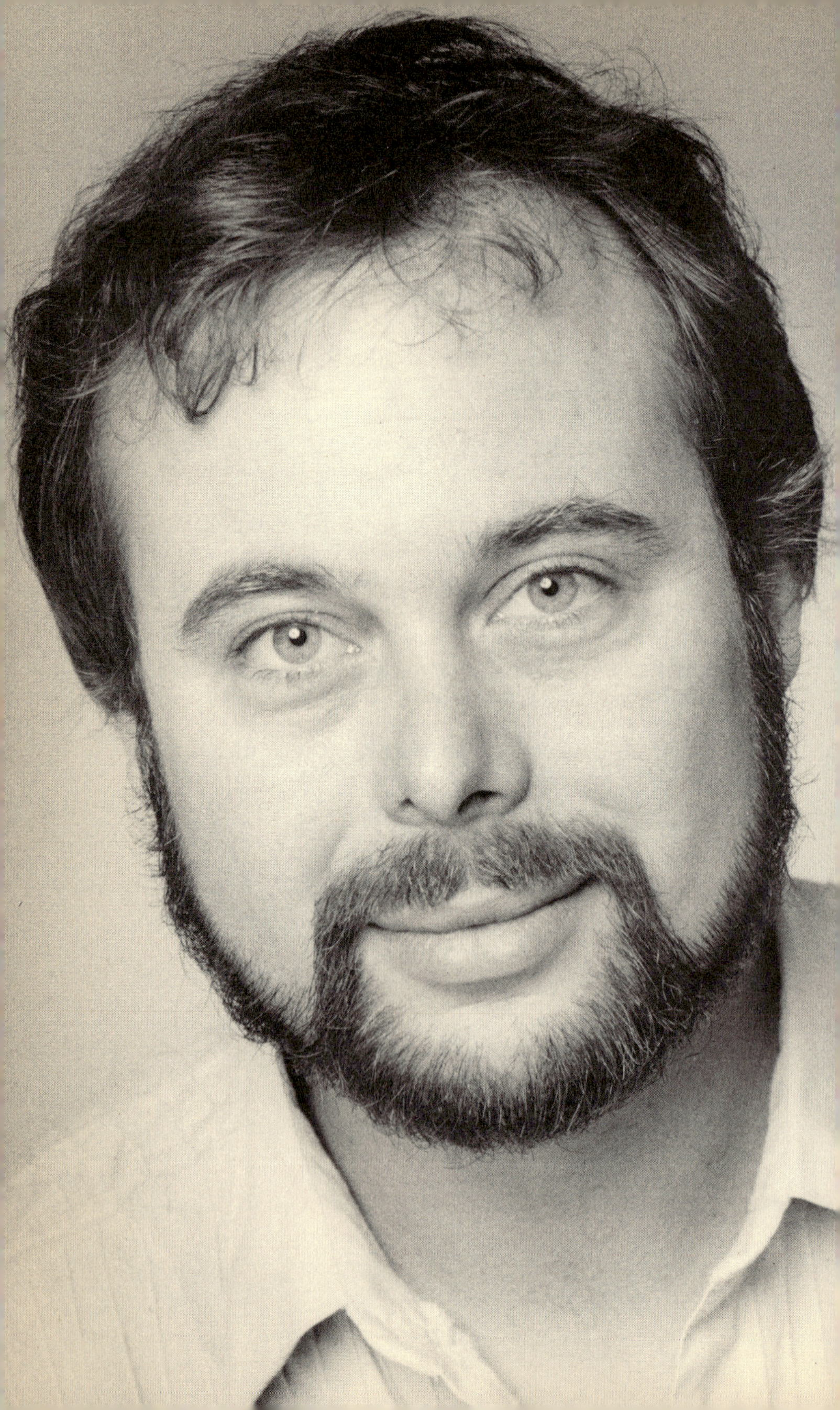

TERRY BURGLER
ARTISTIC DIRECTOR
*THEATRE*VIRGINIA, RICHMOND, VIRGINIA

Terry looked around the elegant room. By training, by background, and by disposition, he ought to be on the *other* side of the table. He ought to be one of his audience—a group of doctors, lawyers, and business people representing the cream of Richmond society. Their long history of family position and commercial success represented a variety of races and religions and an interest in the public good outside their individual fields. That is why they had been asked to become part of the Board of Directors of *Theatre*Virginia, the resident theater company at the Virginia Museum of Fine Arts. Terry Burgler could have been expected to become one of them. Instead he had recently become artistic director of the company, and this was his first meeting with the Board. They were essentially his bosses.

"There were some plays done in my high school. I'm sure there were," he says today. "I think I even went to one or two." But Terry was an athlete and a scholar. He was set to major in English at Princeton University. Theater hadn't even entered his mind.

Terry's father was a computer expert with the Air Force when computers were new and experimental. Most military couples move around frequently, and their children must constantly develop new friends and adjust to new schools and new neighborhoods. Because of Mr. Burgler's specialty, the family lived permanently in Virginia from the time Terry was five through his high-school graduation. That predictability, coupled with a fine innate intelligence, gave the young "jock," as he recalls himself today, a combination of polite self-discipline and assertive self-confidence. He loved to read history—not so much because it was history, but because it was "the best bunch of stories you could get hold of." He also liked to write. He had all the qualities that would have made him a good doctor or lawyer—one who would have made a good member of a board of directors.

At Princeton the creative control of the writer—together with the narrative sense of the historian—manifested themselves in Terry's interest in film. During his first three years he took all the available film courses and "wasted a lot of film on statues and squirrels." But as he learned more about commercial films, he backed away. He did not like the fact that studio executives and editors and sound dubbers and marketing bureaucrats could make decisions that could compromise the artistic quality of a movie. He became jealous of the control that kind of collaboration takes away from the film director. Theater seemed a simpler and more manageable field. He started by acting in three plays with the undergraduate theater at Princeton during his senior year. By graduation time it was clear to Terry that theater would be his career. The excitement of being involved with a play was like what he had felt in high-school sporting events. "Being in an arena and playing a game give an extraordinary excitement to the event." He became a young man with a purpose. The purpose was to become a man of the theater. The practical side of such a decision did not interest him much at the time. He "caught" theater in the way some people catch a cold. "Theater is something you do for theater's sake. It's an old-fashioned career. The people in it create without any particular expectation of legitimate rewards." But "man of the theater" might include any number of different theater jobs.

Terry took classes at Washington's Arena Stage during the summer after his Princeton graduation. Then, in the fall, a friend arranged an interview for him at Stage West in Springfield, Massachusetts. He might become a general intern and have a chance to work in all phases of the operation. He might. But they took someone else with more experience. Terry was disheartened. How would he ever get into the theater if the people already there took all the jobs? Then one of those accidents-that-change-lives happened. Shortly after the Stage West season began, there was a shake-up in the top management, and everyone in the company moved up the ladder a notch. That left an opening at the bottom and Terry climbed on.

Because of the shake-up, the staff at Stage West was thin. Terry did everything. He worked on scenery, he acted, he got the costumer to teach him to sew, he gathered props. Like a sponge, he soaked up everything he could see, hear, or experience, and by the end of the season it was clear to him that he wanted to be a director. Everything about the theater interested him. And the one person in whom everything came together was the director. The level of control and authorship that a director had, appealed to him. His mind was set. Now he would have to set his course for achieving that goal.

Experience was the key. He had so little. Three plays during his senior year at Princeton and a season as an intern did not make for a very full resume. After a summer of acting and running props for a dinner theater, he returned to Stage West as prop master. That gave him an opportunity for direct responsibility. He took his work almost too seriously. When a production of *Hedda Gabler* required a set of academic notes from which the characters are supposed to reconstruct a book, Terry created not only the papers but an elaborate social theory of his own written into the pages. His work was so interesting that one night the actors on stage got involved trying to piece together Terry's ideas and very nearly missed their cues.

Terry soon realized that it was not necessary to be quite so thorough with stage reality. But he also took the experience as a lesson in his own development. He had a good basic education, but it was not a theater education. The disadvantage was that he had to learn for himself many things that formal theater training would have taught him. Ironically, his lack of formal training also was an advantage. By learning on his own, he was free of the built-in prejudices of individual teachers, and he could develop his own viewpoint. The experience itself was his teacher. He understood history and social theory. He now understood how to make a prop. He had gone too far with the *Hedda Gabler* manuscript, but his impulse to keep the prop consistent with the structure of the story was good. Learning to find the balance was important.

During his time at Stage West, Terry lived in his van. His salary was only enough to pay for an apartment *or* to provide a little social life with the rest of the company—not both. By sleeping in the van and showering in the theater he was able to pay for his meals and admission to a movie on his infrequent nights off. He seemed to be living in the theater, and that was fine with him.

Then a remarkable thing happened. Terry was working as a bartender at a restaurant near Washington for the summer in order to stockpile extra money. He knew that the owner had an unused pavilion on the property, and in off times he would talk with the older man about developing a dinner theater there. The idea obviously appealed to the owner, but Terry was totally surprised when the man asked him to set up the operation. Logic said it was impossible. But with the enthusiasm of youth and the energy that comes with personal responsibility, Terry decided he could do it.

He had to start from ground zero. The pavilion was an open shell. Terry had to decide on the arrangement of stage and dressing areas, tables and buffet line, bar and kitchen. He had to choose plays and hire staff. Common sense was his guide, and he learned as he went along. He trusted his instincts and hired people to work for him whom he felt he could trust. The Lazy Susan Dinner Theater was a success from the day it opened. Then another theater in the area hired Terry away, and he took his second job as artistic director for the Moseby Dinner Theater.

Although he had been highly successful, Terry realized that his *real* future lay in noncommercial theater. The regional repertory companies were doing the types of plays he liked, plays which dinner theaters could not handle or would not risk. He also knew that the repertory companies were somewhat snobbish about the more popular dinner theater field. Although he had been lucky and successful, Terry wanted to separate himself from his image as "a man of the *dinner* theater." Graduate school might be an answer. He enrolled at the University of Virginia. He had worked professionally as an actor, technician, director, and producer. Now, at last, he was going to get some formal training for the career he was already pursuing.

After obtaining his master's degree, Terry worked for several theaters before taking a job as associate artistic director at the Virginia Museum. When the artistic director left, the board of directors asked Terry to assume the top position.

One of the primary skills used in his new job is his ability to direct productions. Directing was what first attracted Terry to the theater, and it is an art he has continued to nurture as he has added other skills to his arsenal. As director of a production, Terry must understand both what a script says and what it means. He must control the flow of one scene into the next, and he must establish rhythms and tempos both in the actors and in the scenery and lighting that surround them. Actors and technicians who have worked with Terry praise him highly for his ability to explain an acting moment or a particular technical effect. They sense that he has been there himself and knows their problems and their potential.

As artistic director, Terry's duties go far beyond directing plays. He must help create and maintain a workable budget for an entire year—or "season"—of plays. He must hire the regular staff as well as guest directors and designers. He must match available talent in design, direction, and performance to the productions planned. Most of all, he must maintain an overview of the season as a whole. Terry describes a season at another theater run by another artistic director in which six of seven shows were staged on dark gray sets. It was accidental. Each director had arrived at the choice independently. "But imagine if you were a regular patron watching the sixth drab show. By that time it must have seemed like a statement was being made." Terry believes a good artistic director avoids that kind of accident by planning physical productions along with planning the scripts to be presented.

It is this logic and objectivity that mark a successful artistic director. Yet Terry has not lost his enthusiasm while cultivating his objectivity. Theater is clearly a passion with him, and he gets impatient with people who treat theater timidly. "We're now being so tasteful that the sheer rambunctious energy that is part of theater is starting to fade. Theater is not a passive event. It is an active event. If it's a difference between a bold choice and a tasteful choice, I want people in my theater who'll make the bold choice. There is a danger of theater becoming almost respectable."

Clearly, Terry Burgler is a committed man of the theater. But that commitment has not been without cost. His one marriage has resulted in a separation, in part because of the time and energy he pours into his work. And when asked what he is like outside the theater, he almost stops talking. He mentions a love of nature and of getting away alone to the mountains where he can just watch the drama of the animals and the forest. But the conversation quickly returns to his home base—the theater. "The things I do in my professional career . . . I don't think of it as a professional career. I think that's why we talk of 'a man of the theater.' It's something that's an entire lifestyle. I am what I do. That's who I am."

Terry Burgler (photo on page 48) saw early on that the person in whom all of the theater skills came together was the director. That was who he wanted to be. (Photo by Ron Jennings.)

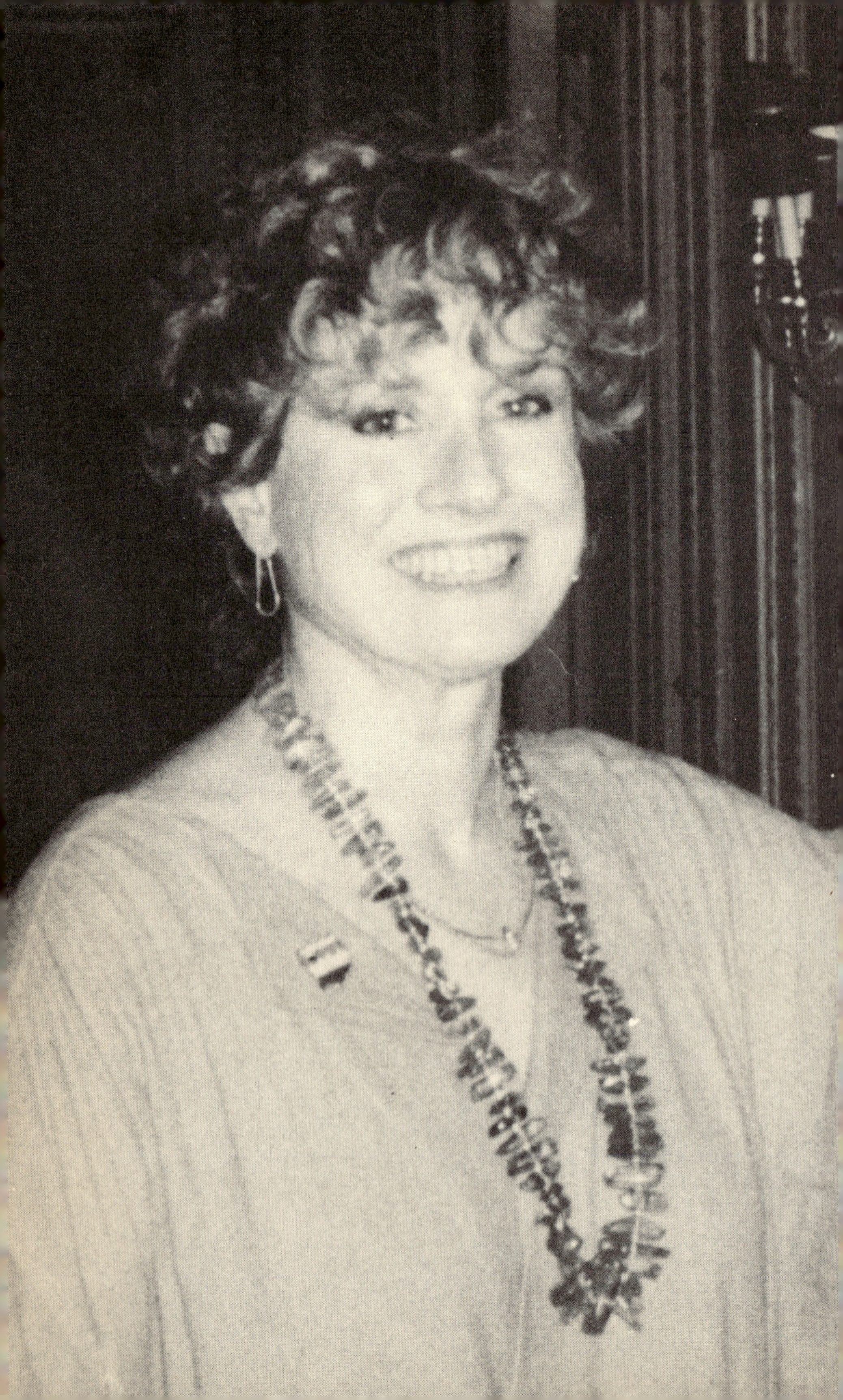

PATRICIA ZIPPRODT
COSTUME DESIGNER
BIG DEAL ON BROADWAY

She arrived for the interview a little late. She had been one of the celebrities asked to appear at a rally to kick off the "Hands Across America" event in New York. On the stage with her had been Helen Hayes, Angela Lansbury, Lily Tomlin, Ben Vereen, Penn and Teller, and a host of Broadway stars. She was as well applauded as some of the more generally known personalities. Did she feel like a celebrity? "Not really. My name is very well known—but by a small group of people." That small group of people has watched with admiration as Patricia Zipprodt has costumed *Pippin, Chicago, Fiddler on the Roof, Cabaret, Zorba, Plaza Suite*, as well as the films *The Graduate* and *1776*. The designs have brought her nine Tony-award nominations and two Tony awards as well as an array of other honors. She is one of only three or four designers who can truly be said to be at the very top of the profession.

In the beautifully appointed parlor of the Dramatists Guild, ten floors above Sardi's restaurant, Ms. Zipprodt talked easily about how she started as a costumer. It is a story full of ironies and accidents. It started in Evanston,

Illinois, with paper dolls. It has come now to her tenth Tony nomination for her recent work on *Sweet Charity*.

As a child she always drew events. Not just pictures—events. There was always action in her art. People were picking flowers. Birds were feeding their young. When she graduated to paper dolls, she would always cut out settings from magazines and dress her paper figures appropriately for going to a party or an afternoon at the races. Visual art was her acknowledged talent, and she was sent to the Art Institute of Chicago for classes, even while she took up some acting in high-school plays. When it was time for college, her first impulse was to continue at the Art Institute. But a wise teacher persuaded her to spend a few years in academia. Her talent would still be there. But she might never again have the chance to read and study the great literature of the world. She chose Wellesley College.

Since she didn't think she would have to depend on her liberal arts education, she was free to enjoy it. She spent four years with books and almost devoted her life to scholarship and social work. But sitting with a friend watching a performance of *La Valse* at the New York City Ballet, her life was changed.

She had graduated from Wellesley and moved to the city for the summer to paint and think about the future. She loved painting but feared the uncertainty of art as a way of life. Watching the ballet she realized that the dancers were wearing skirts composed of layer after layer of silk net—each in a different color. "It was an epiphany!" she says today. "I realized that I could paint with fabric. I suddenly knew that I should be a costumer." The only problem was that she knew almost nothing about making clothes.

At the suggestion of a friend, she enrolled in the Fashion Institute of Technology. The officials there were a bit confused at first since they were used to students who wanted a degree. Pat already had a degree. But she made it clear that she was more interested in what she could learn than in getting a particular piece of paper.

The FIT program was intensive and exacting. They cared little about design. That could come later. They were interested in teaching students the most demanding standards of garment construction. Pat was sure she was in the right place.

She knew she would have to take an examination for the design union. Her training at Wellesley was her salvation. She sat down in the library and taught herself the history of costume. When she achieved a top grade on the union's exam, the officials were confused. She had never had formal training in design. How had she done so well? "It's all there in the books!" she said. Her determination had driven her to use her study skills to further her career.

She then started hounding all the costume designers whose work she admired to allow her to assist them. Some did, and she learned even more. That same tenacity drove her to hound a producer to give her a job as a designer. The play was *The Potting Shed*. It was for Broadway, and since it was a modern-dress show, the producer had not thought much about the costumes. Since this young woman was available and so very interested, she got the job almost as an afterthought.

The Potting Shed was not only Patricia Zipprodt's first Broadway play, it was the first play of any kind she had designed for on her own. She had come into costuming with a full range of disassociated skills. She quickly realized that she had better get some more experience, bring the skills together and focus them, before she came to play again in the big leagues.

Through friends she found work at the Circle in the Square, which had developed a small but interesting theater venture downtown in Greenwich Village. Because she had all the skills necessary to both design and construct, she was valuable to the company and thus was there when Circle in the Square did one of its most famous early productions, *The Blacks*, which turned out to be a landmark event. Most of the more important black actors working today were in that production, at a time when there were few opportunities for black actors anywhere in professional theater. Because it was a significant production, everybody in the theater wanted to see it. When they came, they also saw Pat Zipprodt's costumes, and that eventually opened doors all over town.

She was called by the Phoenix Theater to work for directors like Jerome Robbins and Hal Prince when their careers as directors were just beginning. Later, when they were creating Broadway history with shows like *Fiddler on the Roof* and *Cabaret*, they brought along the costume designer they knew could give them what they wanted: Patricia Zipprodt.

Pat does not talk easily about her style of designing. She is hesitant to label it, for fear that defining it would destroy it. Rather, she concentrates on her good fortune in developing solid technical skills and a practical approach to her work. She credits FIT with the craft and Wellesley with the practicality. And she shares that down-to-earth common sense with students at New York University and Brandeis University when she isn't actually working on a show.

Her Brandeis students got a special treat when *Big Deal* was in Boston trying out. She brought them into the theater to work with her on some of the one hundred costumes that she had designed for the musical. These were graduate students in costume design, and they were going to have a chance to work under top professional conditions. Pat had taught them construction with rigorous standards. She had taught them the process of designing, with its weeks of thought and sketching and talking with the director and the other designers. She had taught them how to budget a show, how to contract with fabric dyers and shoe makers. She had taught them about costume history and the effects of light on various fabric weaves. She had suffered with them through their own productions at the university theater. Now she assigned them the task of taking a set of newly built prisoner costumes, black and white jailbird outfits, and distressing them to look as if they'd been worn for years in a real prison. Dye and paint were hauled into the musty basement of the Boston Shubert Theatre. The student costume assistants scrubbed, patched and roughed up the cloth in an effort to make it look as unappealing as possible. In the dead of winter the theater basement was cold and uncomfortable. At least one rat made an appearance but was offended by the paint smell and left for more accommodating quarters. The work was tedious and dirty, staining hands and clogging nostrils. In the midst of it, Ms. Zipprodt called a temporary halt to the proceedings. "Can anyone tell me the difference between what you're doing here and what you should be doing at the university or at any other theater you work for?" The students stopped and thought. A few wiped their hands of the muck they had been working in. One or two put down needle and thread to pay attention. They had all designed similar outfits. They had all tried to turn directors' ideas into visual images. They had all built pieces perfectly only to turn around and age them. Pat waited a moment before giving them the answer. "The only difference is that this is a five-million-dollar production. And while you might get paid more for working in a production like this, the work itself doesn't get any better."

Patricia Zipprodt doesn't see herself as a celebrity. But framed by the mirror in the parlor of the Dramatists Guild (photo on page 56), she looks very much like a special person.

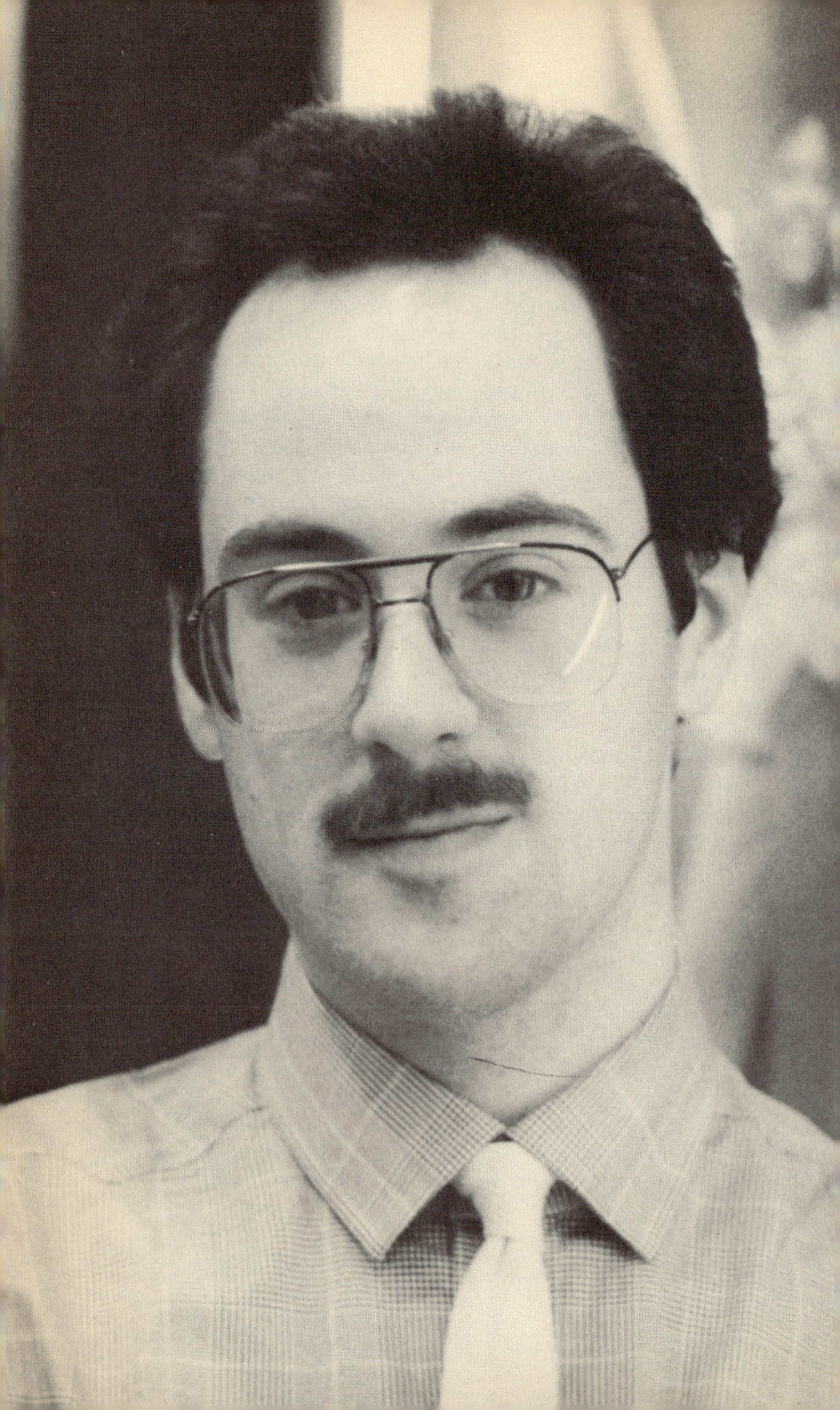

BERT FINK

PRESS AGENT
BIG DEAL ON BROADWAY

Tavern on the Green was alive with light. Perched on the edge of Central Park, the great glass walls of the garden room reflected both the dazzling crystal chandeliers inside and the barely budding trees wrapped in white twinkle lights that surrounded the garden. The light bounced off the perfectly polished bar glasses and the silver serving pieces which held the lavish buffet. The party was sure to be a success.

The guests were as polished and bejeweled as their setting. Black tie was a standard for the men, but it gave way here and there to personal interpretations. Here a man was wearing an open silk shirt. There, another was all in velvet. The ladies were just as individual with their colors and fabrics and ornaments. These were not people who followed fashion. These were people who made it. They were the cast and friends of the Broadway show *Big Deal*, and they were here on this April night for their opening-night party.

The parking lot was filled with limousines, and the chauffeurs leaned on the fenders of their elaborate cars and chatted with each other. Just inside the door an area had been set up for the press, and strobe flashes could be seen from time to time through the windows. Bob Fosse, the legendary director of the show, was having his picture taken with Dustin Hoffman, with Loretta Devine and Cleavant Derricks who starred in the show, with Gwen Verdon, rock superstar Patti LaBelle, and with the other celebrities who had been invited to help make the occasion as festive and special as possible.

In the midst of this excitement Bert Fink tried to remain calm as he hurried from table to table greeting, congratulating, inviting first this celebrated face and now that distinguished person to step out to have a picture taken. He kept an eye on the bar and on the food table, making sure that everyone was well fed. Someone needed an extra copy of the program, and he just happened to have one. Someone asked about a copy of a picture from the lobby, and Bert told him to call the office the next day. Earlier he and his boss, Fred Nathan, had herded the photographers down the aisle at the beginning of the curtain call for this opening performance so that they could record the actors in the flush of their anticipated triumph. Now he was making sure these photographers had a chance to see and chat with as many of the luminaries as possible. And whenever anyone asked him, "Any word on the reviews?" he would smile and shake his head and change the subject. He already knew about the reviews, but he didn't want to say anything now. This was a party. This was a time for fun and celebration. This was no time to tell these performers, who had put their heart and soul into the past five months of work, rehearsals, frustration, joy, and hope that the reviews were, almost without exception, bad.

Bert Fink grew up in Barrington, Rhode Island. He played with toy theaters as a child, and his parents were Gilbert and Sullivan fans. At the age of nine he saw his first Broadway show—*1776*—and he fell in love. He asked for a copy of the album, and he played it night and day for months. He began to collect pictures and articles and books about theater. Something wonderful had happened to him. He wasn't quite sure what it was, and he wasn't quite sure where it would lead, but he was very sure that he wanted to spend his life on Broadway. It was not so much theater as an institution that he loved. Rather it was the magic and mystery of Broadway. It was liner notes from albums of Broadway musicals. It was souvenir programs and pictures clipped from magazines. It was the excitement of opening night and the sense of being close to the stars who make up the electric-lit sky over Times Square. Bert Fink had an itch that could be scratched only by a job of some sort close to the Broadway stage.

In high school Bert's proudest memory came from taking his class to see the touring production of *Pippin*. He had played the record for a year. He had told the story and shown the pictures he had collected. He had passed around the articles and write-ups he had clipped, and now he was able to host his class when they all went as a group to see the show. Small, with no interest or ability in sports or other school activities, Bert was finally able to share with his classmates something that made him feel special. And his friends responded. They enjoyed the event. They saw some of what made the little guy tick. It was a great evening.

During college at SUNY (State University of New York) at Purchase, just outside the city, Bert spent every weekend in Manhattan seeing shows and writing reviews for his college newspaper. Some of the more "serious" theater students objected to the fact that he didn't review the drab dark dramas that they thought worthy of "serious" consideration by any "serious" student of the stage. But Bert followed his own instincts and his own tastes. He loved Broadway. He would write about Broadway.

When he graduated from SUNY in June of 1982, he moved in with his grandmother, who lived in Westchester County. The move kept him close to the city. He spent the summer exploring the city and interviewing with every theater business office he could find. The differences between producers and general management firms, advertising agencies, and press agencies were still blurred in Bert's mind, and he still did not have a fix on the exact nature of his ideal job. As a result he interviewed with all kinds of companies, hoping as much for the experience of meeting people as for an offer of work.

It was during that summer of exploration that Bert first sat across the street from the Winter Garden theater and watched as sign painters on hanging scaffolds turned the block-long billboard on the front of the theater into a poster for the upcoming production of *Cats*. The sign, almost as large as a football field, was covered in black. Then two huge yellow eyes appeared with the black profiles of dancers as pupils. It was a startling design. It was dramatic and glamorous and dynamic and everything that Broadway ought to be. As Bert sat in the plaza of the Uris Building and munched on his street-vendor hot dog, he wondered if he would ever be a part of that world of drama and glamor and excitement. Less than a year later he was working for the press agent who represented many of the top shows on Broadway, and his first assignment was, of all things, *Cats*.

When Bert first called the Fred Nathan office it was just another in a long list a friend had xeroxed from a professional contact book. Anne Abrams answered the phone, and the energetic young voice on the other end asked her about the possibility of an interview. To get rid of him she said, "We're right in the middle of a big opening. Call me next week if you're still interested." She thought she would never hear from him again. But the following week he called again. She set up a time to see him. "When he first called I figured he was just making the rounds to see if we had any openings," said Anne some time later. "But when he called back the next week, I figured he was serious." Anne was then an assistant to Mr. Nathan, and when Bert sat down she was charmed by his freshness and obvious enthusiasm for the Broadway arena. He showed her a portfolio of his reviews from his college paper and various articles and clippings he had either written or helped get published. They talked for a while, and then she said, "Now let me give you two free lessons." Bert was galvanized. "First," she said, "You handed me the portfolio and looked out the window while I went through it. You should be doing the work. You should be selling yourself." Bert saw immediately the difference between an active interview and a passive one. "Next," she said, and Bert listened attentively, "I mentioned I had a friend in the Shubert office and I paused. You should have immediately asked for the name." Bert was learning. The Fred Nathan office didn't have any openings just then, but Bert's interview with Anne Abrams had turned out to be a valuable step in his development.

Broadway doesn't have the luxury of an elaborate screening process. Because budgets are always tight and because there are always more people willing to work than there are jobs to fill, most people get hired on instinct rather than on a time-consuming series of contacts. Unfortunately, those who get hired one day can just as easily get fired the next. In Bert's case, it was more than six months before Fred Nathan came out of his office one day and told Anne Abrams he needed another assistant. Bert had taken Anne's advice and used it well when he had interviewed for another company that didn't have any openings either. But it just so happened that Fred called the person

Bert had interviewed with for a recommendation, and between her positive reaction and Anne's instinct, Bert was offered a job with the Fred Nathan Company in February of 1983.

Officially Bert Fink is in the process of serving an apprenticeship with the Fred Nathan Company before ATPAM, the Association of Theatrical Press Agents and Managers, will qualify him as a fully credentialed press agent. As an apprentice/assistant he has had the opportunity to work on *Cats*, *Private Lives* with Richard Burton and Elizabeth Taylor, *Zorba* with Anthony Quinn, *Noises Off*, *Sunday in the Park with George*, and many other notable Broadway successes and failures. In the three years that he has been with the company, his work has become noticeable to the small family of theatrical business people who make up the little world that is Broadway.

It can be an isolated world at times. In a recent interview Bert described his reaction when he turned on the television on the evening of April 14, 1986, to find that the United States had completed a bombing raid on Libya. "It's a little embarrassing," said Bert, "but the first thing I thought of when I heard about the Libya raid was, 'Will this affect "The Today Show"?' I had Loretta Devine and Cleavant Derricks from *Big Deal* scheduled for the next morning, and I was afraid all the news coverage would push them off the schedule." He was right. Late that evening the producer of the NBC morning program called to say that they would have to reschedule the appearance. Bert then had to call the two stars and tell them, as well as the musicians who were to back them up when they sang a song on the air. That is the kind of thing a press agent does. He had set up the piece initially by convincing the producer that the two Broadway stars performing one of the songs from the show would make an appropriate spot for the early-hour television audience. Once the date was set, he checked with the musical director of *Big Deal* to decide which song to do and how many musicians would be required. He arranged for the musicians, checked out the copyright on the song to make sure that the appropriate fee would be paid for broadcasting it, and notified several press outlets that the guest spot was about to happen. When the piece had to be canceled because of the pressure of world events, he had to reverse that same process and retract all that information.

A theatrical press agent is employed by a show both to handle requests for information and to generate interest in the show. Much of the work of the press agent is standardized. When a show is about to go into rehearsal and again when the show is about to open, the press agent prepares a press release giving general details such as who wrote the show, who is directing, who the stars are, when the show will perform and where. Next come photographs of the show. The press agent engages the photographer and sets up photo calls. He then has the pictures reproduced and sends them out to a long list of newspapers, magazines, and other press outlets. He also begins to select photos that will be enlarged and used in the lobby and in front of the theater to excite passersby. There is also the souvenir program full of photos, as well as photos in the regular program. Each actor submits biographical information, and the press agent edits that down into useable shape for the programs. He then goes about the business of answering specific requests for interviews and photographic shoots. Before a show opens, most of the media set up cameras in isolated positions and take footage to be used with television reviews or features on shows like "Entertainment Tonight." Opening night is an especially busy time for the press agent. Each of the critics has been invited and sent tickets. As they arrive the press agent must make sure they are seated properly and have any additional pictures and information they need. Yet he must never seem to be trying to influence a review or favor one critic over another. If special guests are expected at a performance, celebrities or friends of the producer or director, the press agent will sometimes act as host. He also acts as host for the opening-night party and other social events given in honor of the production. During all this, the press agent is keeping a record of every mention of the show in the press, every picture printed, and every media event that carries the name of the show he works for.

What Bert Fink discovered after going to work as a press agent was that this was the very job he had spent his whole life preparing for. His writings about shows, his collecting of clippings and pictures, his desire to meet and know the people of Broadway had found the ideal setting in the Fred Nathan office, and because of that, most of the time Bert Fink is a contented young man. But not always.

The opening night party for *Big Deal* at Tavern on the Green had gone on until 2 AM. When word got around that the reviews were bad, the party thinned out a bit. But a few revelers held on, determined to make the best of a disappointing situation. Bert saw the last party guest to the door of the restaurant and thanked the manager as he locked the front door. In the cool April-night air he tried to piece together what the coming days would be like. He had worked on one show that had closed on opening night because of bad reviews. He hoped that this one would not repeat that process. It was hard to face the actors and the other creative people who had put so much time and effort and hope and love into a project and watch their stricken faces as the words "we are closing the show" are spoken. There was a meeting scheduled for 10:00 in the morning. It would all be sorted out there.

It is an irony and a mystery and part of the magic that

is Broadway that if that 10:00 AM meeting had been held on schedule, *Big Deal* might have posted its closing notice that day. But early Friday, Fred Nathan called Bert and said that the meeting had been postponed until 1:00 in the afternoon. Bert spent the morning assuming the worst and headed for the producer's office in a state of controlled depression. By the time he got there, everyone was smiling with guarded optimism. Despite the reviews, the telephone business had been brisk that day. There was a line at the box office, and by noon the show was taking in $10,000 an hour. There was an audience out there that wanted to see *Big Deal*. They had heard about the show. They had heard about the actors and the fact that Bob Fosse was back on Broadway. They didn't care what the critics thought. They wanted to see a big, splashy, glamorous, exciting Broadway show, and the negative viewpoint of the "serious" reviewers was not going to keep them from it.

Bert Fink had done his job. He had helped make the public aware of the wonder that is Broadway. He had made the title *Big Deal* part of the current public consciousness. Few of those people standing in line for tickets knew it, but they were there, in part, because of Bert Fink. That's the kind of work that can make a person very proud.

Bert watched them paint the block-long billboard for Cats *not knowing if he'd ever break into show business. Less than a year later he was working for the show. (Photo, page 62, by George Storey)*

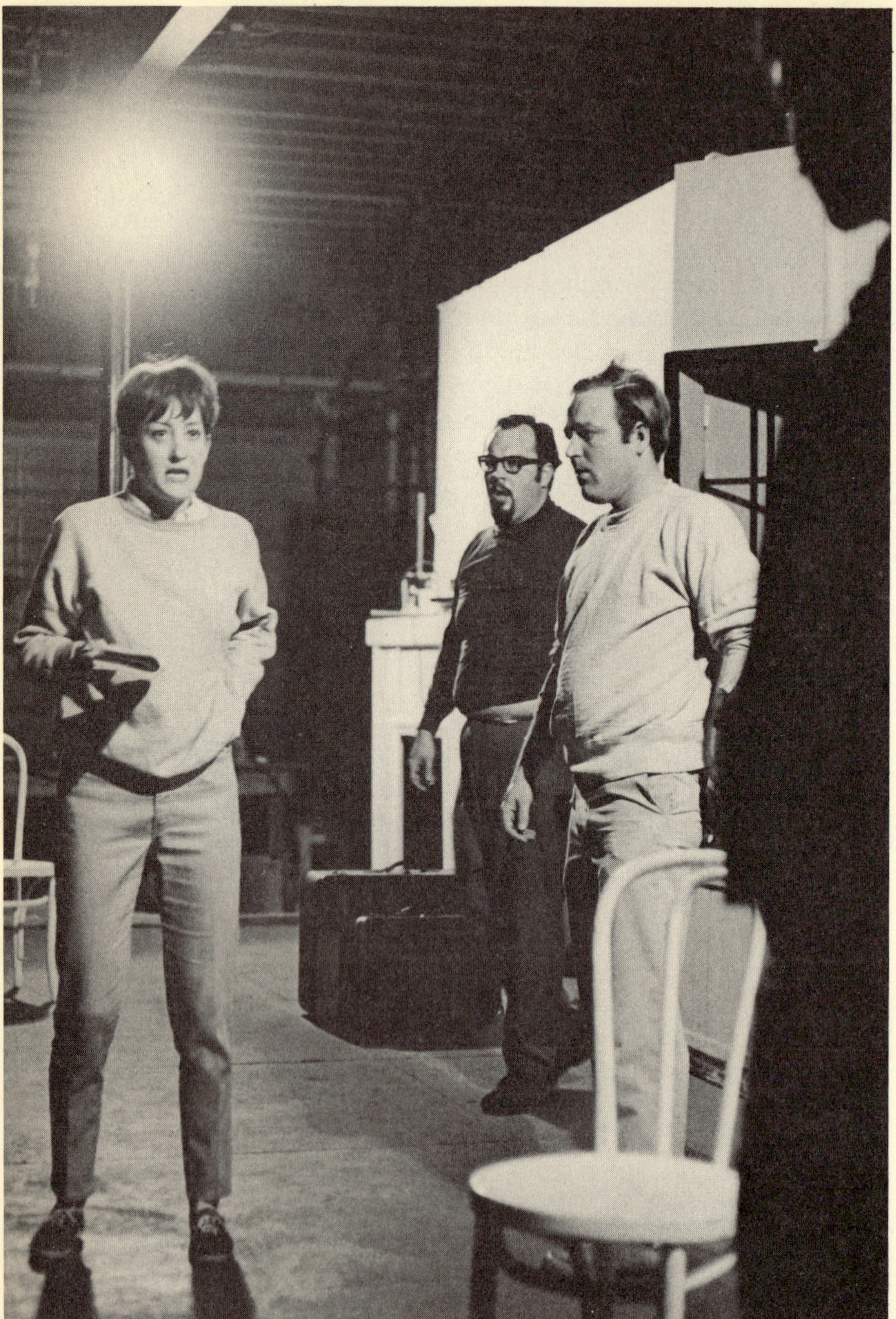

CREATING THE PRODUCTION 73

Many people think of the production beginning when the actors begin rehearsal. (Here a dinner theater production of The Knack rehearses with studio chairs and scripts in hand.)

Planning the production, however, has been going on for some time. Much of that planning takes place at meetings like this one at which director and designers go over the script carefully and discuss the needs of the play and the style of the production.

Page Two

EXPENSES

Scenery
Design	2,000
Construction	5,000 —*Revise down*
Prop, Purchase	1,000

Costumes
Shopper	1,000
Purchases	1,000

Lighting
Design	5,000 —*Revise down*
Purchases and Rentals	10,000

Performance Personel
Actor (2 weeks pre-opening x 500.)	1,000
Stage Manager (2 x 500.)	1,000
ASM Understudy (2 x 400.)	800
Tech Assistant (2 x 400.)	800
Lighting Technician	400

(Figures include Insurance, FICA, etc.)

Administrative
General Manager	5,000
Office Expenses	2,500
Legal Fees	7,500
Press Agent	5,000

Production
Take In (Cartage and Extra Hands)	3,000
Theater Deposit and Use	10,000
Preliminary Box Office	3,000
Insurance	5,000
AEA Deposit (Bond)	3,000
Printing and Promotion	10,000
Photos and Signs	5,000
Radio, T.V. and Print Ads	25,000 —*Revise up*

CREATING THE PRODUCTION 75

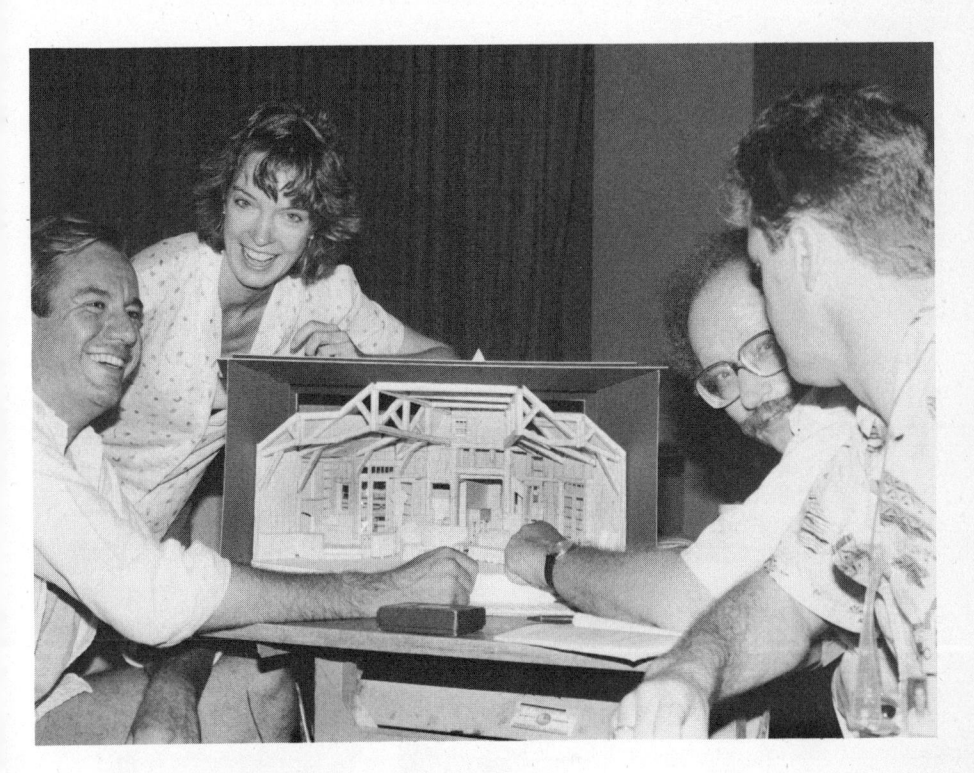

A scale model of the set, which the designer builds, is a great help to actors and directors in seeing just how the environment for the play works before the scenery is actually built.

One of the primary considerations of any production is "How much will it cost?" (This preliminary budget is for an off-Broadway production of The Gospel According To Saint Luke. The play uses one actor in one costume on one simple set. It is projected to cost just over $100,000 before opening night.)

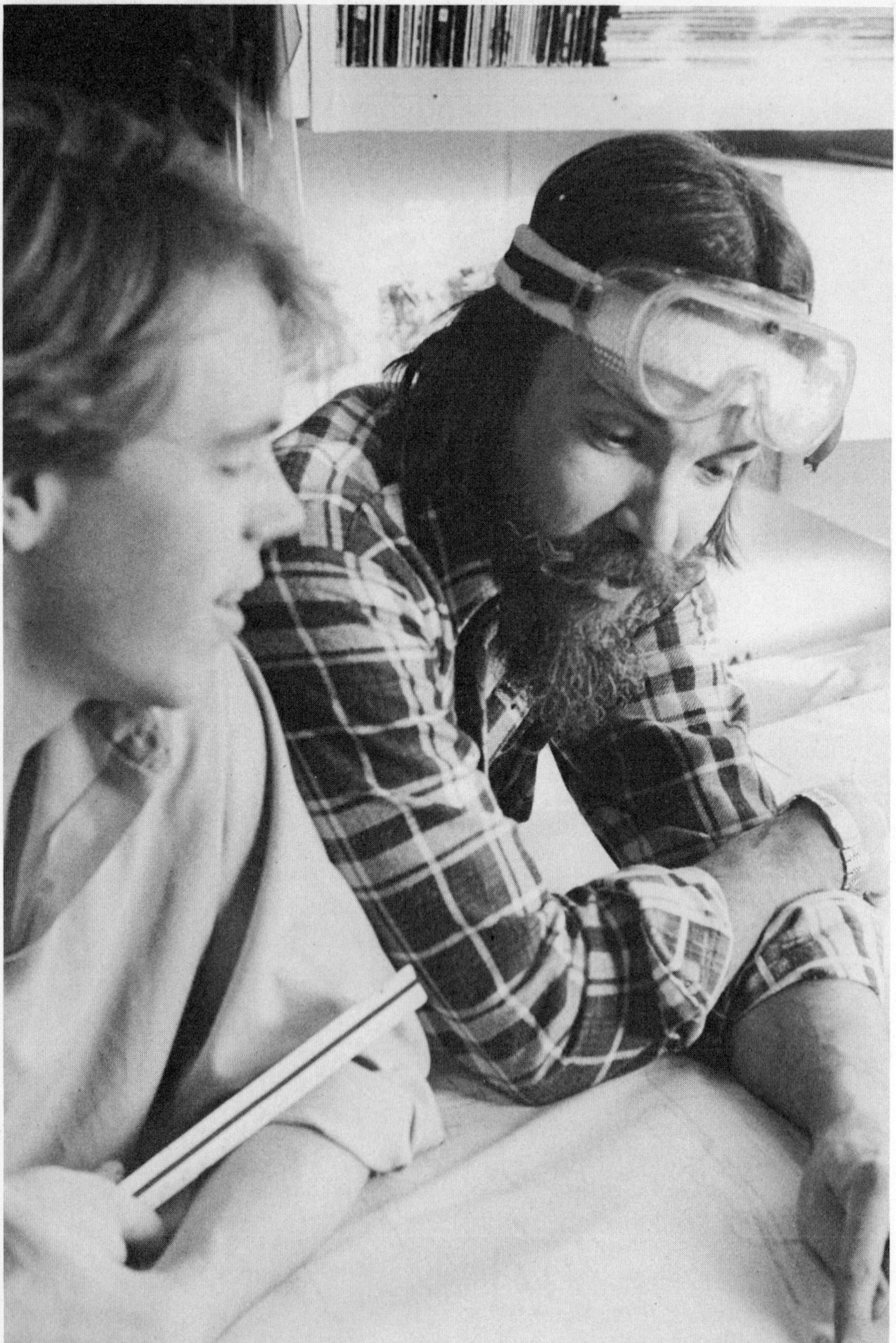

CREATING THE PRODUCTION 77

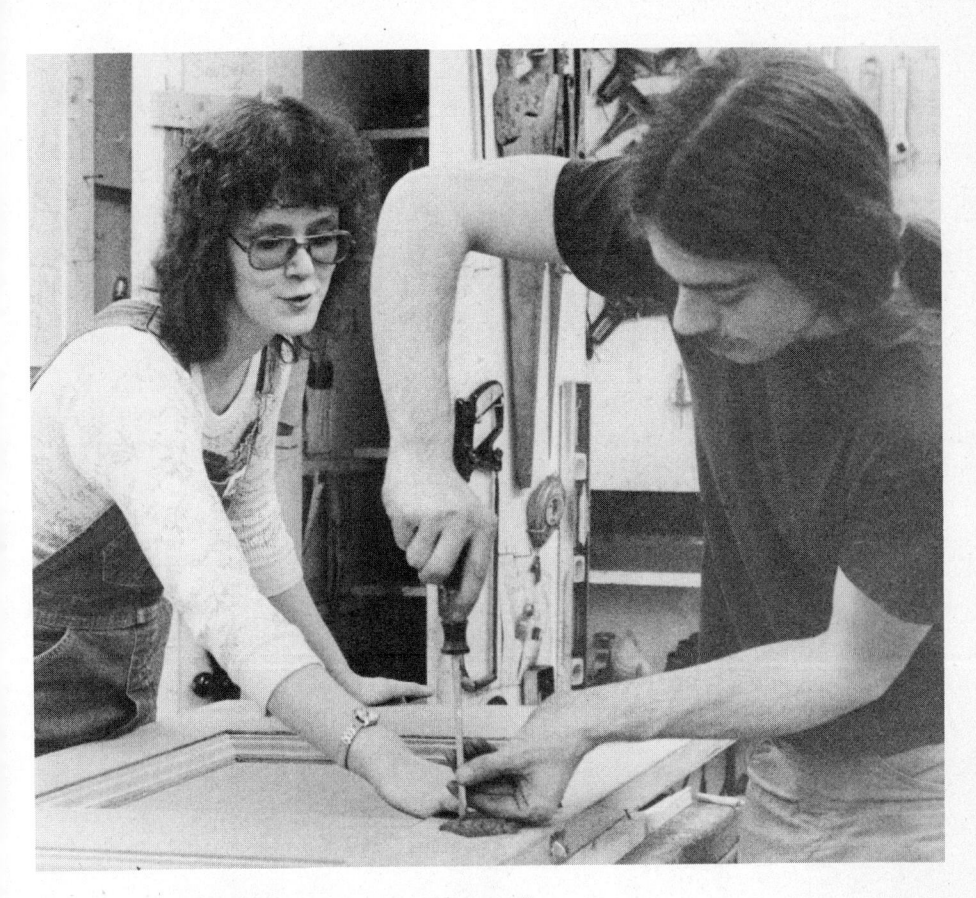

The technicians who will build the set must have blueprints of every piece of scenery they will construct. The set designer draws them up, but the technicians must know how to read them.

Whether they are called stagehands, crew or scenic technicians, the people who build the set and props for a production must have a variety of mechanical and woodworking skills. Traditionally, scenery is built from wood and canvas.

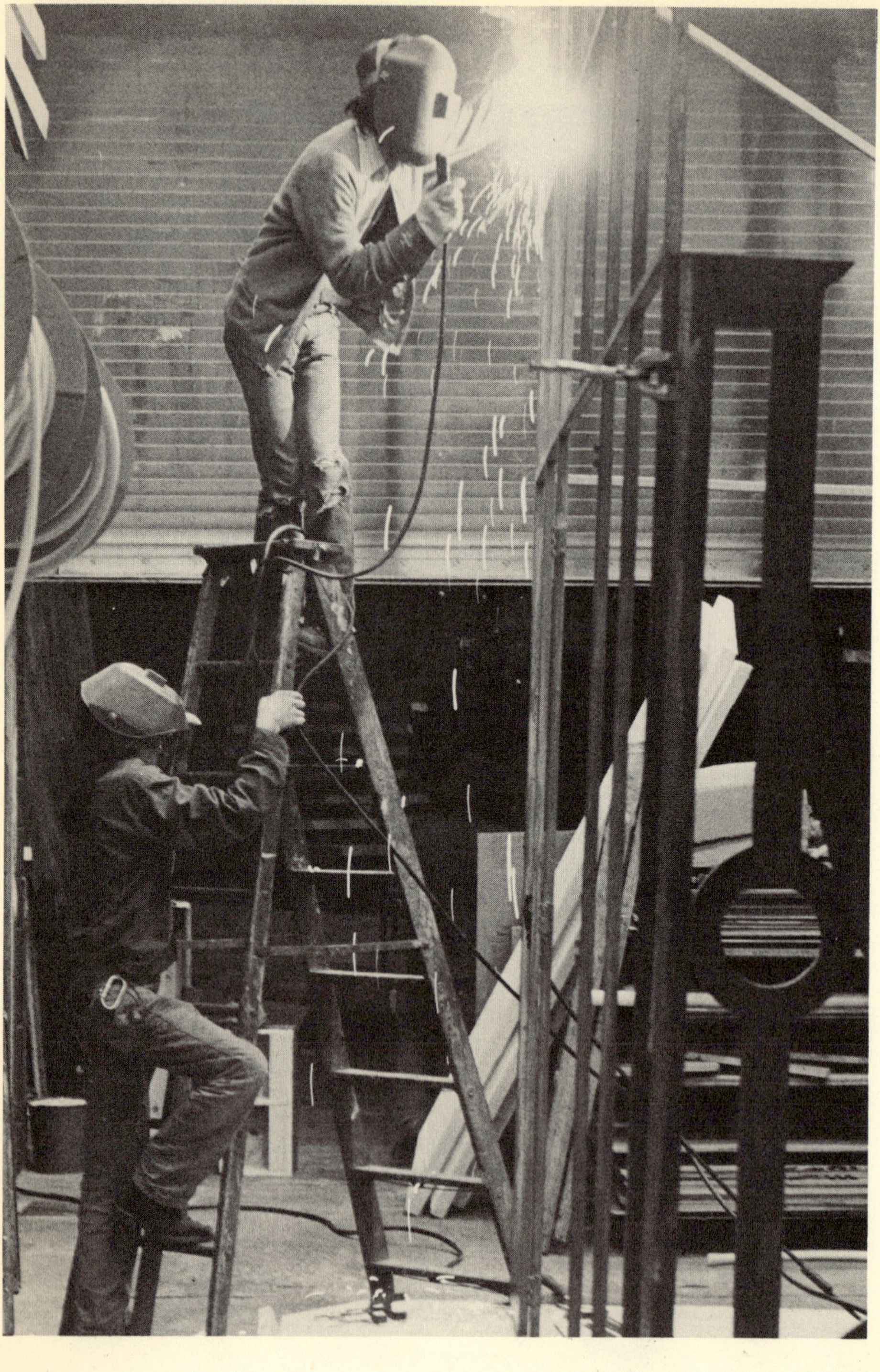

Modern designs, however, require all kinds of construction techniques.

The modern scenic shop contains all the equipment found in any mechanical shop and must be maintained in a clean and orderly manner. This applies to everything from accurate blue-

prints to sweeping up daily. Training for scenic work is not unlike the training offered in industrial classes or technical schools.

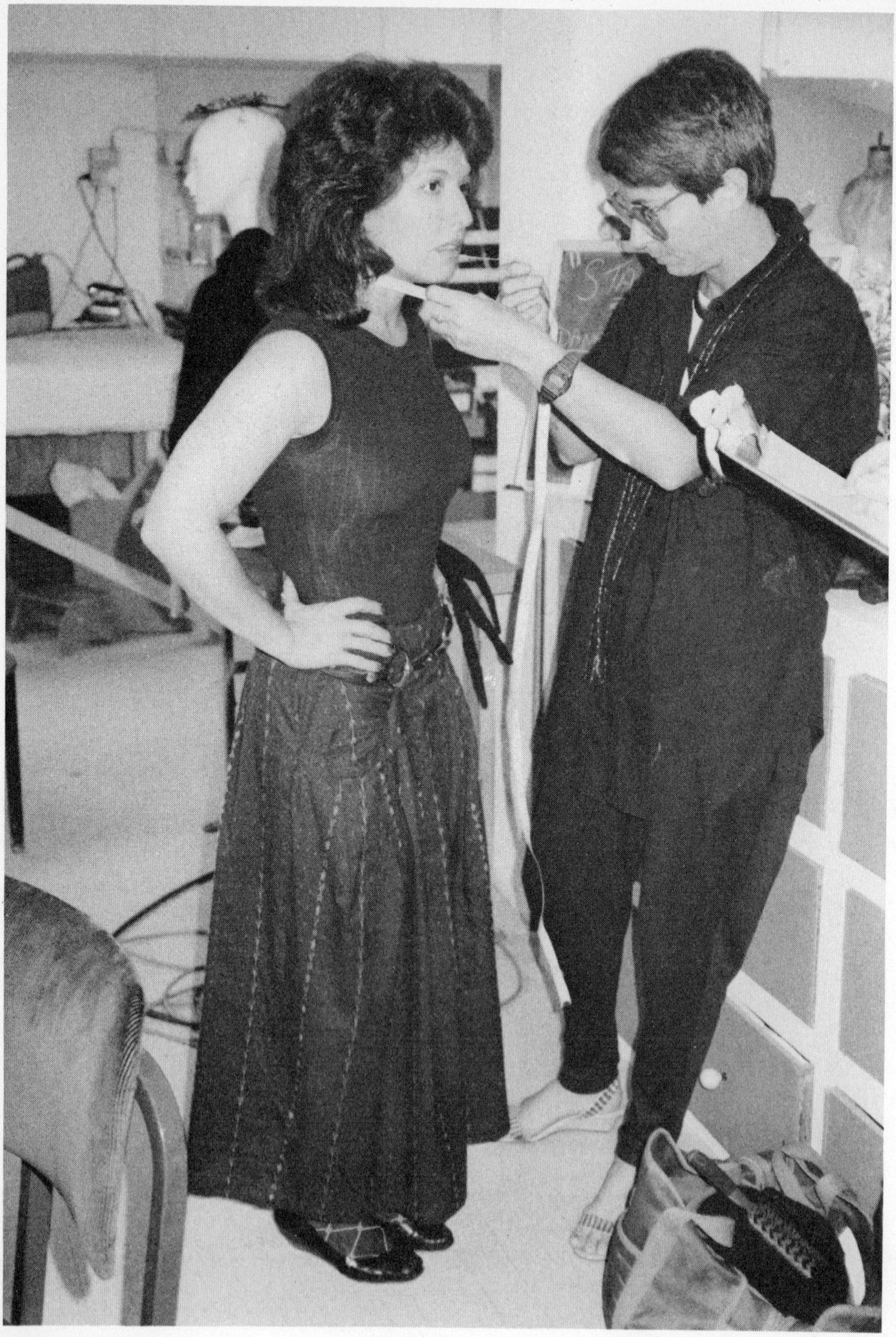

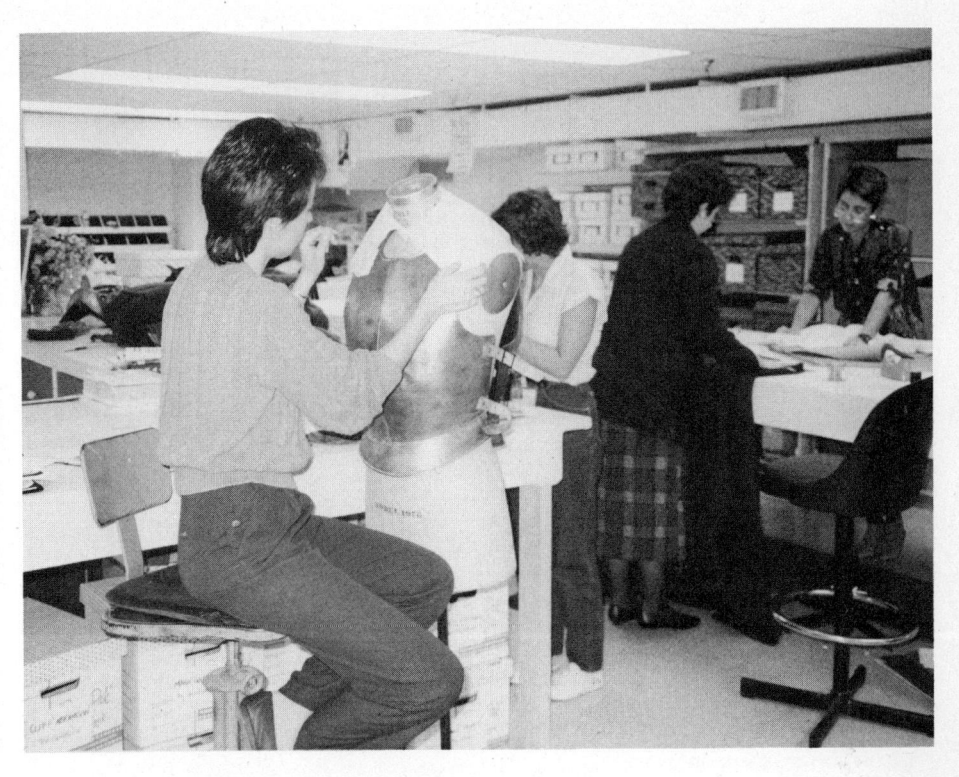

A costumer must be prepared to work with anything from ordinary street clothing to stage armor.

Costumers, too, must have a variety of skills beyond sewing. (Here a TheatreVirginia costume staffer takes measurements from an actress in a new production.)

LUCIEN DOUGLAS

AEA AFTRA SAG   (212) JU2-4240

Ht - 6'0"
Wt - 160
Hair - brn
Eyes - hazel-brn

THEATRE

MEDEA
  Broadway
  Kennedy Center
	Jason's Messenger	w/Zoe Caldwell
		Judith Anderson
		dir/Robert Whitehead

NAKED FAMILY BUSINESS CANDIDA Roundabout Theatre, NYC	Franco David Lexy	 dir/John Stix dir/Harold J. Kennedy
THE DINING ROOM MACBETH THE HIDING PLACE (premiere) A CHRISTMAS CAROL Virginia Museum Theatre	Actor 3 Malcolm Duncan Ruyker Fred	 w/Alfred Drake
THE HEIRESS AS YOU LIKE IT MERCHANT OF VENICE ARSENIC & OLD LACE Clarence Brown Co, Knoxville	Morris Townsend Orlando Bassanio Mortimer Brewster	 prod/Ralph G. Allen
VIRTUE REWARDED THE TEMPEST The Players, NYC	Paolino, lead Ferdinand	dir/Alfred Drake w/Alexander Scourby

FILM & TELEVISION

MEDEA	Jason's Messenger	PBS/Broadway Prodn.
GLORIOUS SYSTEM OF THINGS PBS/Colonial Williamsburg Found.	Peter Littlefield, lead	cast/Shirley Rich
THE GRIMKE SISTERS PBS/Secondari Productions	Henry Grimke	cast/Shirley Rich w/Dianne Wiest
ANOTHER WORLD	Assistant D.A.	NBC

COMMERCIAL

On-camera & Voice-over (Breakstone, Consolidated Cigar, Korvettes...)
THE ETERNAL LIGHT, NBC radio

TRAINING

Royal Academy of Dramatic Art, London
Univ. of Conn, BFA
Douglass Watson, master class

LUCIEN DOUGLAS

While technicians usually sign on at one theater for an entire season of productions, actors travel from theater to theater and from role to role. (Actor Lucien Douglas uses this picture and resume to pass out to directors at auditions and to send to directors who may be looking for someone with his look and experience. A director looking at this resume would notice that Lucien has worked on Broadway, has worked with several distinguished directors and is usually cast in roles that require a bit of classical style.)

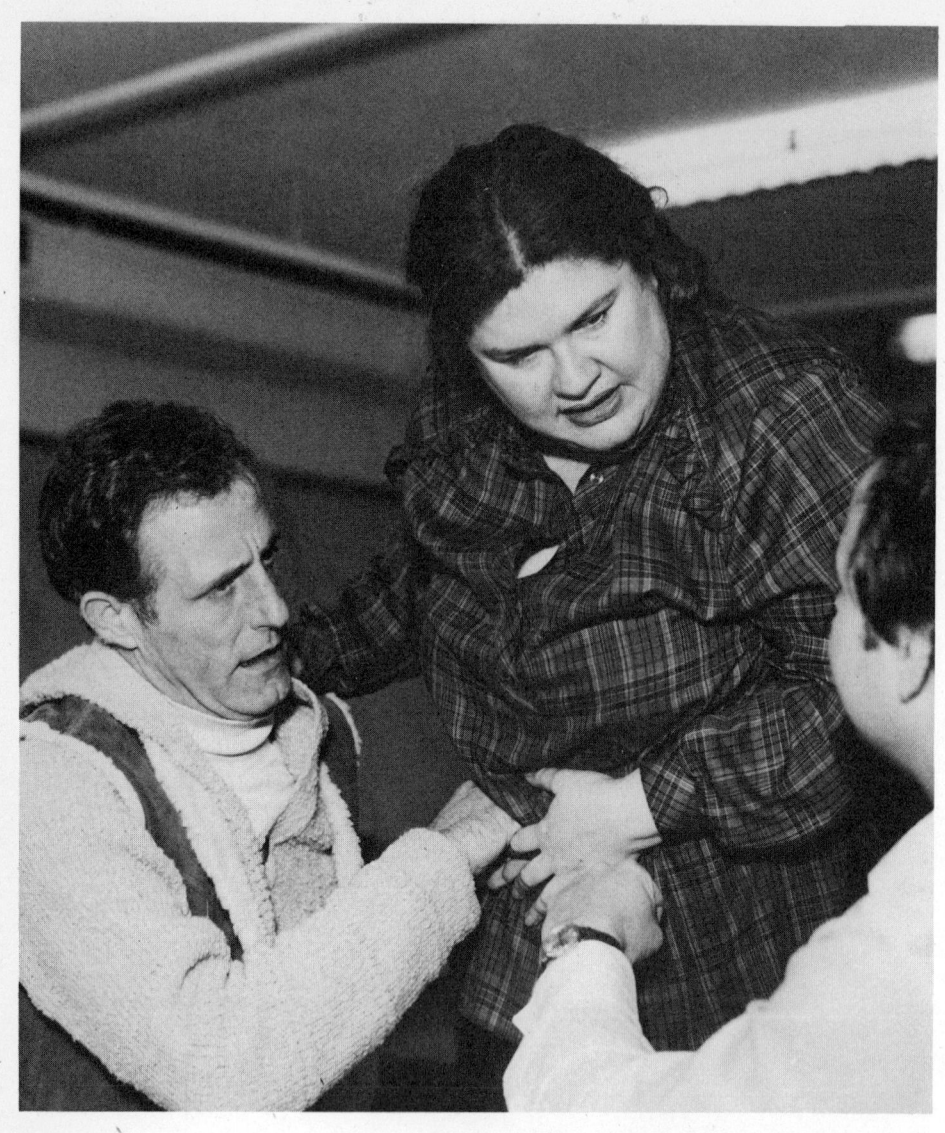

Actors depend on the director both for information about the characters they are playing and to be a "third eye"—an objective viewer of how their work looks from out front. (Here director Terry Burgler works with actors Judith Drake and David Gale in the TheatreVirginia production of The Sea Horse.*)*

The stage manager (Jane Page, seated) is the primary assistant to the director and a major resource for the actors (Judith Drake L. and David Gale R.). The prompt book which the stage manager keeps details every move and cue, and many of the director's notes.

Ultimately, however, the actors must work out many pieces of stage business on their own. (Judith Drake and David Gale work out a move in the Theatre Virginia *production of* The Sea Horse.*)*

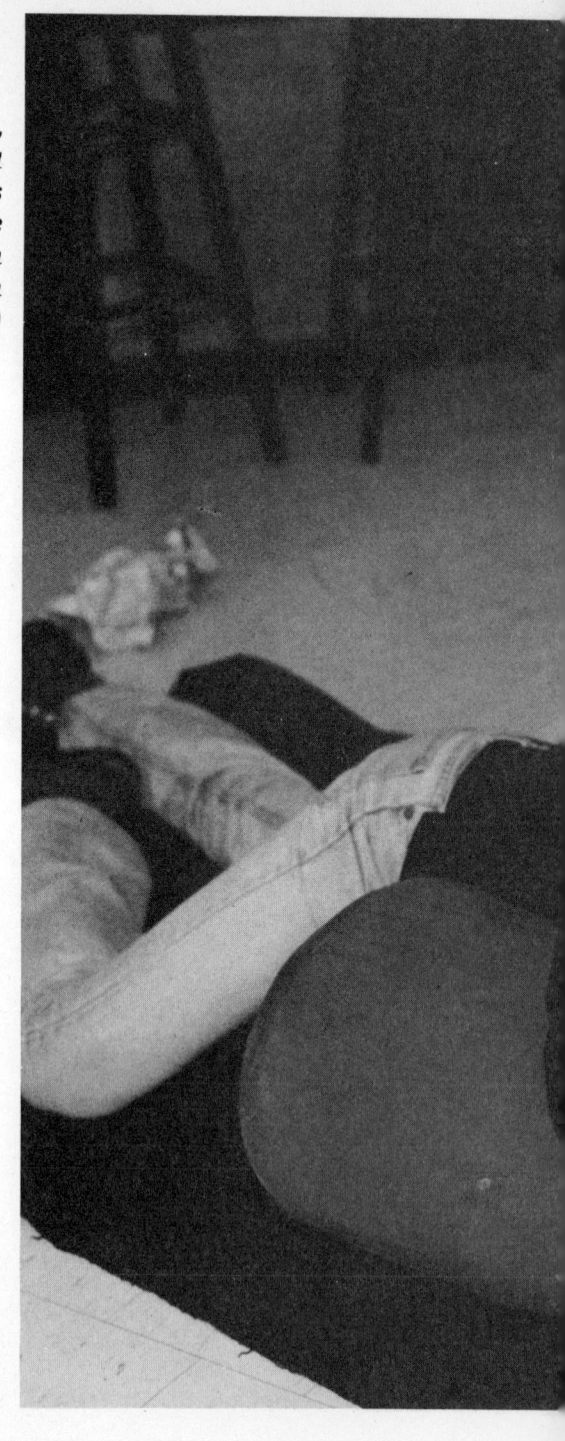

(Photo Credits: 1, 3, from the author's collection; 2, 4, 5, 6, 7, 8, 9, 10, 13, 14, 15, courtesy of TheatreVirginia; 11, 12, courtesy of Lucien Douglas.)

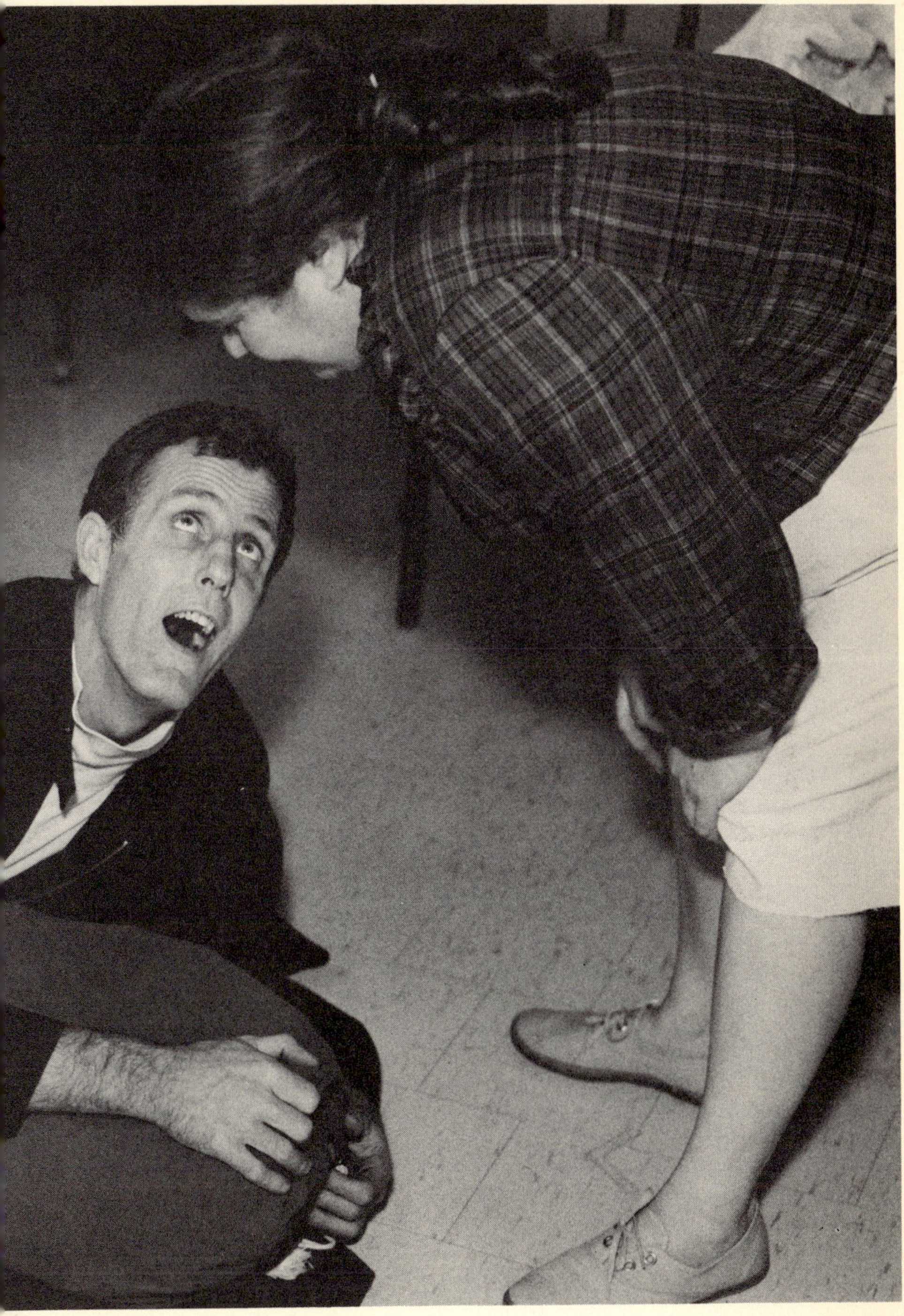

SECTION III
RUNNING THE PERFORMANCE

There may be no more powerful, exciting, and evocative phrase in our language than the term "Opening Night." Imagine, if you will, the animated crowd gathered under the brilliantly lighted marquee. Imagine the approach of the huge black limousines. Imagine the glittering audience, ladies in furs and jewels, men startling in the simplicity and elegance of their tuxedos. Imagine the rush to find seats under the spectacular crystal chandelier. Imagine the tense hush as the house lights dim and the great velvet curtain begins to rise. Opening Night is here!

In fact, not all opening nights are so elaborate or so costly. Not every theater has a chandelier. Not every audience has the chauffeur or the formal garb to make the first night of a play as much of an event as the one described above. Yet, whether it happens in the stately glamor of a Broadway house or in the more rustic confines of Harry's Dinner Playhouse in Smallville, opening nights are always exciting, because with the opening of the play comes the beginning of the *magic,* and it is the magic of the theater that makes the magic of opening night possible.

And now the show is open and running. For eight performances each week, audiences file into the theater. Some have read reviews. Some have seen advertisements or feature articles. Most have heard from friends that the play is worth seeing. Word of mouth is always the best advertisement.

It is often said that the show is now in the hands of the actors. But it is also in the hands of a small army of technicians who operate scenery, run lights and sound, place props, and make sure that the actors are in the right costumes. There are also ushers and house managers and box-office clerks and custodians who keep the front of the house running as smoothly as the performance.

Some of the technicians first joined the company in the shops where scenery and costumes were being built. There are "show" technicians hired by the producer, and there are "shop" workers who are employed by the shop which has been hired to do the construction work. The "show" workers move to the theater with the scenery and costumes, lighting equipment and props. There they are joined by other "hands" who are hired strictly to run the performances. All these technicians are supervised by the stage manager who has been with the actors since rehearsals began. The front-of-the-house staff is supervised by the general manager and the company manager, as well as by the theater manager who works for the owner of the building.

The four technicians presented here are all with the Broadway production of *Big River*. *Big River* is a musical dramatization of Mark Twain's *Huckleberry Finn*. In this case the project was the idea of the producer, Rocco Landesman. Mr. Landesman and his wife were attending a concert by country-rock musician Roger Miller. In the taxi after the concert, Landesman mentioned to his wife that Miller's music would be a perfect complement to

Twain's famous story. The Landesmans convinced Miller and then began to put the show together. The first production was at the American Repertory Theatre in Cambridge, Massachusetts, some two years later. That production was followed by another in California. Most of the California company came to New York with the show.

Each of the four people we are about to visit came to *Big River* from a wide background of talents and experiences. Yet at every performance their focus is the same. They work to help make the magic happen between the actors and the audience.

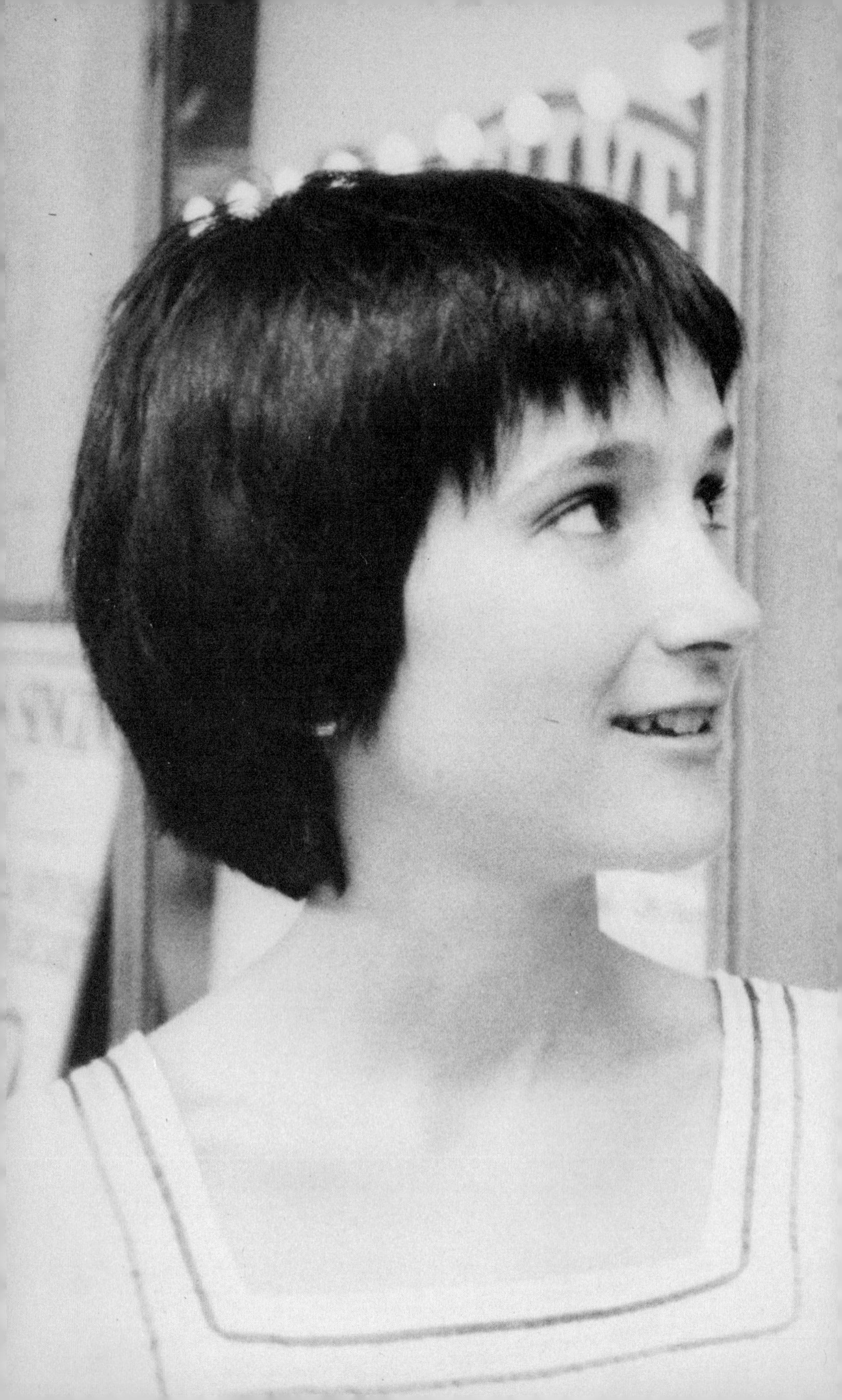

MARIANNE CANE

ASSISTANT STAGE MANAGER
BIG RIVER ON BROADWAY

The actor was droning on and on about spending his days doing commercials and parts on soap operas and how much more money that paid than this work. This work was the role he was playing eight times a week in *Big River*, one of the biggest musical successes on Broadway in many years. The actor and his audience were sitting in the Eugene O'Neill Theatre. The audience he was speaking to was a group of high-school students who had arranged with the show's press people to talk to one of the actors after a matinee performance. The actor was impressing them with numbers and percentages and displaying a thorough knowledge of the *business* of acting. But he was describing theater only in money terms, and that disturbed Marianne Cane.

Marianne was sitting off to one side. She had to wait through this "seminar." As assistant stage manager for the show, that was her job. But she didn't have to like it. Theater meant a lot more to her than the money. The fact was that unless you were working on Broadway, as she was now, there wasn't a lot of money. There were long hours that limited your social life. There was a lot of sweat and concentration and sometimes there was abuse from surly stagehands who refused to take seriously any orders they might get from this tiny young woman. But Marianne Cane has "paid her dues." She has worked her way up in the professional theater and earned the right to hold her own opinions, even if this cynical actor might think of them as idealistic and romantic.

Marianne has proven her ability time and time again. It is Marianne who conducts the weekly rehearsals for the understudies, and when replacement actors come into the company, it is Marianne who teaches them their roles in the show. And why not? She has been with this production since it began at the La Jolla Playhouse in San Diego, California. But Marianne's experience goes back considerably further.

Growing up in California, Marianne found herself fascinated by the magical feeling created when theater lights dimmed and curtains and scenery moved. Her high-school auditorium served as a community hall for dance performances, operas, plays, lectures, concerts. When she found that most of the crews for these events were students like herself, she applied for work and was accepted.

At UCLA she had the opportunity to stage-manage productions from first rehearsal all the way to performance. She expanded her knowledge of stage engineering. She also met Chris Fielder. He, too, was a stage manager/technician with a background not unlike Marianne's. Soon after they had both graduated from UCLA, they were married.

The couple spent another year in California. But they were anxious to go east to New York where there was more demand for theater skills than in California, where most of the work revolved around the film and television industry.

Through friends they found work at Manhattan Theatre

Club, a complex of off-Broadway theaters and workshop studios in the city. There both Chris and Marianne worked as technicians, using all the skills they had developed in both their formal training and in their actual experiences. After the first year they were invited to come back to California for the opening season of the La Jolla Playhouse in San Diego. La Jolla was mounting a summer season, and a pattern was quickly established whereby the couple spent the winter season in New York and the summer in La Jolla.

It was during the second summer at La Jolla that Des McAnuff, the director of the theater, asked them to decide who wanted to do which of the two major musicals of the season. Chris chose to do Randy Newman's *Maybe I'm Doing It Wrong*. Marianne had heard about the musical version of Mark Twain's *Huckleberry Finn* called *Big River* and chose to work as an assistant on that show. *Maybe I'm Doing It Wrong* went on to an extended run in Los Angeles. *Big River* went on to New York.

Since Monday is a "dark" night on Broadway (no performances), Marianne's week begins Tuesday afternoon when she reports to the theater. She and the other three stage managers must make certain that any repair notes given the technicians over the weekend have been attended to. They also check ongoing maintenance and supplies. They make sure that the mechanical aspects of the set have been oiled and cleaned properly and that props that get used up, such as food and chemicals for the smoke machines, have been reordered. Frank Hartenstein, the production stage manager, is Marianne's immediate boss, and Frank goes over the assignments for the week with his staff. Steven Adler and Neal Jones finish the team of stage managers, and their work outside the actual performances is as varied as it is unsung. Several different kinds of rehearsals may be called during any given week. There are the understudies who must be prepared to go on if a regular actor cannot. Some are members of the cast playing smaller roles. Some are hired only to understudy. Then there are brush-up rehearsals called by the musical director or the dance captain when a particular number is in danger of losing the precision that was designed into it by the director. There are working sessions for new actors going into the show to replace actors leaving to take other jobs. There are also replacement rehearsals with the whole cast when these actors are finally ready to perform.

Marianne usually is assigned to teach replacements their roles. She has been with the show longer than anyone on the production staff, having started with it in California, and she can describe the movements, both on stage and behind the scenes, of every actor in the show. *Big River* uses a cast of only two dozen actors to play several dozen characters. Therefore Marianne spends as much time teaching new actors what they have to do offstage as what they have to do on. She carefully shows them when they add a mustache or give a body microphone away. She also has to train them in the traffic patterns they must follow backstage in order to avoid running directly into scenery coming onstage as they are exiting. The actors are often relieved to get in front of the audience, since most of their performing is far less complicated and confusing than the work they do in the wings.

Marianne and the other three stage managers usually rotate assignments during performances. It takes three of them to actually run the show, with one at the stage manager's desk on a platform above the stage and one on each side of the stage floor. The fourth position is usually taken up with special work. When Marianne has a replacement going in, she usually stays backstage to help the actor through the first few performances. One of the stage managers acts as an understudy and occasionally has to be on stage. Frequently one will sit in the audience to take notes on the show and how it is going. Everyone stays busy.

When Marianne is assigned the job of watching from out front, she often thinks about how her career has developed. She and her husband Chris have done very well, and they work often, either together or in different productions. They share a great love for the work they do and a respect for the theater as an institution and as a home. "I believe that all the technical parts are there to serve the performers," said Marianne recently. "That's my focus—making sure the actors can do their best and not have to worry about anything else." Yet, when asked, she laughs easily at the kind of mistake that can be made. Like the understudy who was going on in the lead role of Huck Finn while Dan Jenkins, the usual lead, went on vacation. She had carefully shown him how to make a move in the dark from where he exited on stage right to a position marked by glo-tape on the edge of the stage down left. He was to find his glo-tape marks and stand there, ready to jump down into the aisle of the theater when the lights came up. Unfortunately, there was a man sitting in the front row wearing a dark shirt with bright white epaulets on the shoulders, and in the dark the actor mistook them for his marks. When the lights came up, he jumped directly into the gentleman's lap. The situation was saved by the actor's concern for the man and the man's good humor about the mistake. The audience, knowing that the actor was playing the role for the first time, was enchanted. Marianne was proud that the actor felt comfortable enough with the role she had taught him to stop the action to make sure the man wasn't hurt before continuing the play. Even in the midst of a mistake, she could feel that she had done a good job. Marianne likes to do a good job and has no ambitions beyond the work she is doing now. There isn't often a lot of money, and the hours are long. No one goes home from the theater wondering who was responsible for the play running smoothly, so there is very little glamor attached to the work. But Marianne is philosophical about her position. "You have to know what you care about and why you're doing it. Especially backstage. You have to know it's because you like it, because you like the people, because you think the plays you're doing are important. Because it's something you do really well. And," she adds with a bright smile that recognizes the cynicism and ego that sometimes infect people in the theater, "It's OK to do it because you really love it."

In the photo on page 94, Marianne Cane looks at the posters in front of the Eugene O'Neill Theatre. Both of the actors pictured are replacements. Marianne taught them their roles. (Photo by George Storey)

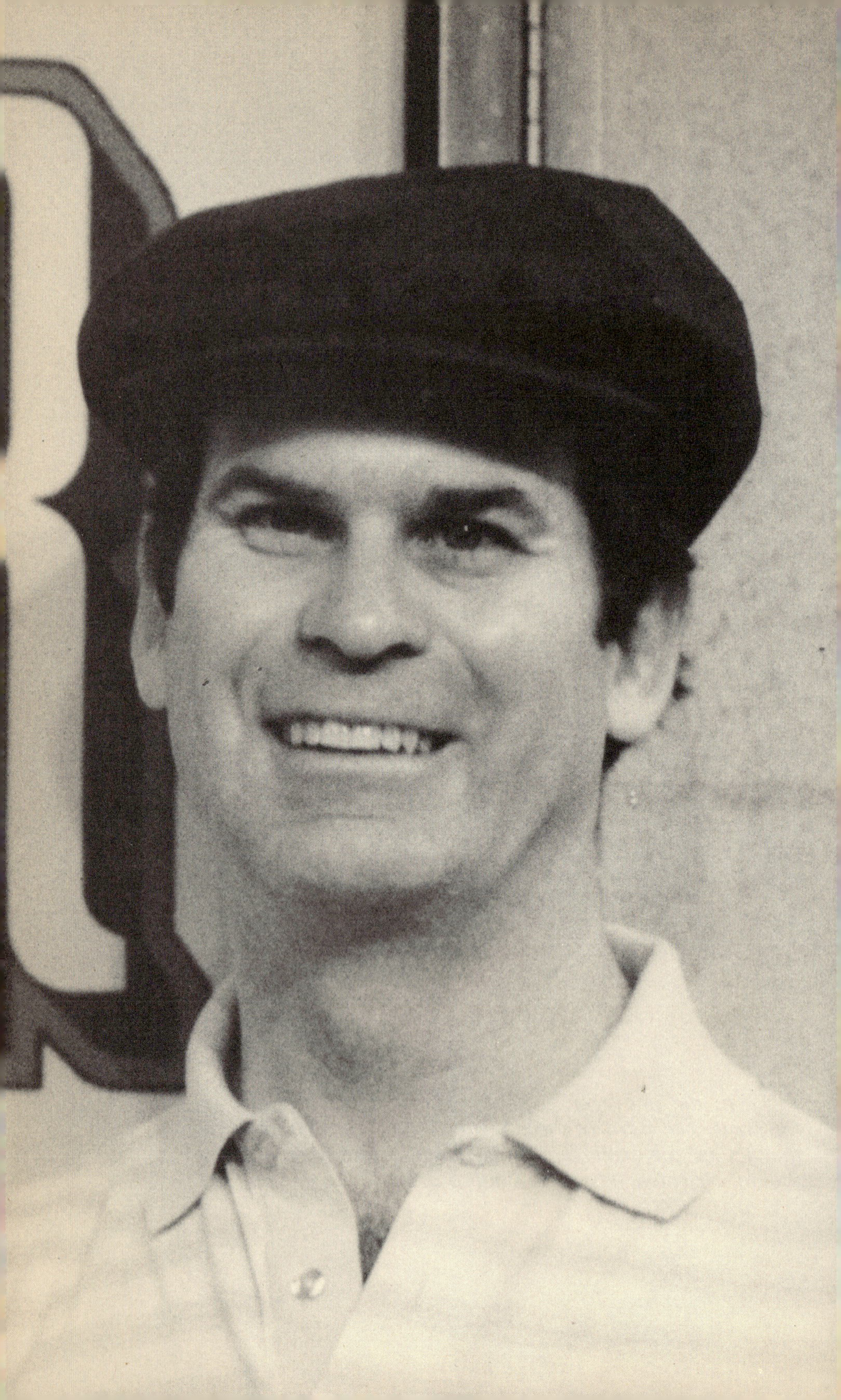

KEITH ELROD

MASTER ELECTRICIAN
BIG RIVER ON BROADWAY

Stop!

He didn't say it, but the word rang in his head like a church bell gone wild: Stop! Stop!

On the video screen in front of him, Keith Elrod watched as the infrared camera showed him that the banquet table, a major prop about seven feet wide, had moved past its assigned position and was finally coming to rest several feet left of where it should be. "Off spike" is the term used when a piece of scenery is not on the mark, or spike, assigned to it. But this piece was not just a little off spike. This was clearly going to cause problems. There was movement and dance all around the table during the next number, and the actors were obviously going to have to compensate to an enormous extent either to keep from banging into the walls or falling into the orchestra pit. And as master electrician for the Broadway production of *Big River*, Keith was responsible for the machinery that ran the banquet table.

Most people think of an electrician in terms of lights and other visible electrical fixtures. In the theater the electrician handles any item that is powered by electricity. And on complex automated shows like *Big River*, much of the scenery is moved by winches that are electrically run. Therefore, although the scenery itself falls under the direction of the master carpenter, the machinery that moves it is in the hands of the electrician.

In this case the table was on a platform that fit into a groove in the false floor of the stage. Inside the groove, cables ran from one side of the stage to the other. Ideally, on a cue from the stage manager, the electrician operating the console that controlled the cables would set the appropriate winch in gear, and the platform would begin to move. The electrician, stationed in the basement of the theater under the stage, had a video screen with marks on it, so that as he watched the table magically glide to its mark on the television, he would cut the power to the winch. This time something went wrong. Keith Elrod would have to find out who wasn't paying attention.

Keith's primary function is to operate the computerized light board that controls some 350 instruments through 230 light changes during the course of the two-hour show. Ironically, he too is fed information by a video screen. The show is so big, and the Eugene O'Neill Theatre is so small compared to some of the Broadway houses, that the only place to put the control equipment was on a catwalk one floor above the stage. From that position Keith is able to see only a limited slice of the stage itself by looking down between the arches of scenery that frame the set. But he remains in contact with the production with both the infrared video system that lets him see the stage even when the lights are not on, and through a headset system with which the numerous stationary technicians have voice contact with the stage manager and with each other.

Keith supervises a crew of nine. There are the four follow-spot operators and two sound technicians who handle both recorded sounds, such as bird calls, and the subtle miking of the entire stage that "sweetens" the volume and balance of the acoustical aspects of the show. There is also a technician who handles the wireless body mikes that most of the principal performers wear, and a deck electrician who works with electrified set pieces and props. And, of course, there is the operator of the winch console. It is standard theater wisdom that the only difference between the stage of today and the stage of Shakespeare's day is electricity. It is standard practice in the lease arrangement between the theater owner and the producer that the producer pays the electric bill.

Unlike most of the technicians who operate Broadway shows, Keith Elrod is not a native New Yorker. He was, in fact, born in Athens, Georgia. While he was still in high school he began volunteering at his local civic theater. He built scenery, hung lights, and operated simple versions of the automated equipment he runs today. By the time he was ready for college, he had decided that he wanted to stay in theater for the rest of his life. He was not aggressive by nature. He did not wear his emotions on his sleeve as many people involved in stage work did. But he enjoyed being near those people, and he enjoyed watching the emotion generated in the audience by the plays he helped perform. The safe shadows of the backstage area seemed a good meeting ground for the quiet nature of the man and the explosive nature of the projects he was working on.

At the University of Florida, Keith studied technical theater, directing, and stage management. He distinguished himself to the point of visibility, and when the people from Walt Disney World came looking for technicians, Keith was recruited into the Disney organization directly after graduation.

Working at Disney World in Orlando involved a variety

of assignments. There were the famous automated shows performed by animated figures styled to portray presidents of history and characters from fiction. There were live shows within the various pavilions, and there were group performances outside under the warm Florida sun.

After a year and a half, Keith decided to move on, and he spent the next few years in stock and regional theater, where he worked on a variety of productions with a variety of levels of technical sophistication. At Disney World he had worked with the very latest in computerized equipment. A single move of a single switch could accomplish hundreds of individualized electronic changes in as many different instruments and machines simultaneously. In some of these new situations, Keith was frequently back to running almost everything by hand. All the same, concepts of organization and technical support for performers learned in the more advanced realm of automation helped him maintain a high degree of professionalism in all his work. When a Broadway touring company came through Orlando where he was working as house electrician for the civic auditorium, they recognized an experienced professional and signed him up to finish the tour with them. This finally landed him in New York.

A series of Broadway shows followed, and Keith was working on *Brighton Beach Memoirs* when Robert Fehribach asked him to work with him on the new show that became *Big River*. Keith and Bob Fehribach are both part of what Keith calls "a small family" of technicians who make up the supervising crews on most major New York productions. The manner in which Keith was hired is instructive in understanding how this family works.

Most technicians get hired on the basis of their reputations. Producers and general managers keep a list of the supervising carpenters and electricians they have worked with before and liked. Dodger Productions had selected

Bob Fehribach as its production electrician, and Bob, who had worked with Keith before, brought him into the project. The production electrician is responsible to the producers and to the lighting designer to see that the designs are carried out accurately and economically. As master electrician, Keith is in charge of the actual running of the equipment and the cueing of the show. These supervising positions are contracted directly to the producers on an International Contract provided by IATSE, the International Alliance of Theatrical Stage Employees. They operate in the same way they would on tour in that the supervising positions are not required to be filled by New York stagehands. The rest of the crew, however, comes from Local 1 of IATSE, perhaps the most difficult of all the theatrical unions to gain membership in.

Richard Riddell was the lighting designer for *Big River*. He based his lights on the set designs of Heidi Landesman and on joint discussions with Ms. Landesman and the director, Des McAnuff. It was Riddell who determined that certain instruments would hit the stage from certain directions with certain color filters and certain intensities in order to enhance the look of the scenery and the mood of each scene. All of that was incorporated into drawings and specifications called a "plot." Bob Fehribach then took the plot and turned it into lists of equipment. He had to survey the theater to see what hanging positions were already in place and what positions would have to be created out of pipe and clamps set into the walls of the theater or hung above the audience.

At that point Keith came into the picture. In the shop where the equipment was assembled, Keith and Bob determined how many lengths of electrical cable would be necessary to operate the show, how many instruments, lamps, color frames, clamps, pipes, and plugs would be necessary to turn Riddell's drawings into a visual reality. Then each piece had to be labeled and listed and packed for the move into the theater. Broadway theaters do not have their own equipment, and most rental contracts work on what is called a "four walls" basis—the stage is assumed to be a hollow shell. Every piece of scenic and lighting equipment must be leased and brought in from outside, and a weekly rental is paid for as long as the show runs. If a show is a great success and runs for many years, this rental fee pays for the equipment many times over. But if the show is a flop, it is considered practical to rent rather than invest hundreds of thousands of dollars in equipment that would then have to be disposed of.

"Put-In" day for a Broadway show is the day on which all of the physical hardware of the production comes into the theater. Dozens of trucks may be required to bring in scenery, platforms, properties, sound and lighting equipment, costumes, etc., and people who work in the Times Square area are accustomed to sidewalks filled with thousands of feet of cable neatly stacked in coils bristling with label tags, or passing between speaker cabinets and wardrobe baskets in order to get to the coffee shop down the block. Dozens of men and women attend this process and carry tons of material from the trucks to the sidewalks to the stage during the course of setting up a show. For *Big River*, Keith Elrod was one of the people giving orders for which piece came through the loading door when.

After the show is installed, the process of setting cues is the next major project. Each lighting instrument is patched into one of several dozen dimmer circuits. During any given scene, the levels of these dimmers may change several times. The decisions about when to change them were made by the designer, the director, the stage manager, and the production electrician. The recording of these cues and their execution is Keith's job.

Once a show is running, the hectic pace of the days

before opening night lightens a bit, and Keith has time for golf near his Rockland County home just outside the city. He also likes to ski and is one of the few sportsmen who books his leisure time on Mondays rather than on weekends. Monday is a day off, and Broadway is dark.

Yet there was one Monday when Keith Elrod felt involved in the show even though it was supposed to be his holiday. On the evening of June 2, 1985, Richard Riddell was given a Tony award, Broadway's highest honor, for the lighting for *Big River*. Keith Elrod was proud indeed. He was being told that the work he was doing was appreciated and admired by the whole theater community.

Sturdy but trim, Keith Elrod has a gracious smile and a gentle manner that is at once friendly and reserved. In conversation he can fill in the details of a union contract or a technical question quickly and with obvious professional skill. At the same time, his personality seems to withdraw when asked to talk about himself and his feelings. Perhaps it is an inborn sense of privacy. Or perhaps it is simply a reflection of the style with which he and others like him must do their work. It is what they do with cables and spotlights and microphones and the computer discs that run them that matters—not the feelings of the operator or whatever poise or charm he may or may not have.

Still, Keith is willing to offer a bit of advice to young people thinking about going into his field. "Volunteer at your local community theater. Ask questions. Don't be afraid to find out more about it. Get involved." For Keith Elrod, getting involved has led to a fascinating life in the heart of one of the toughest and most demanding arenas anywhere—the Broadway stage.

Keith Elrod does a lot more than turn lights on and off (see photo on page 102). His work involves everything electrical on the stage. (Photo by George Storey)

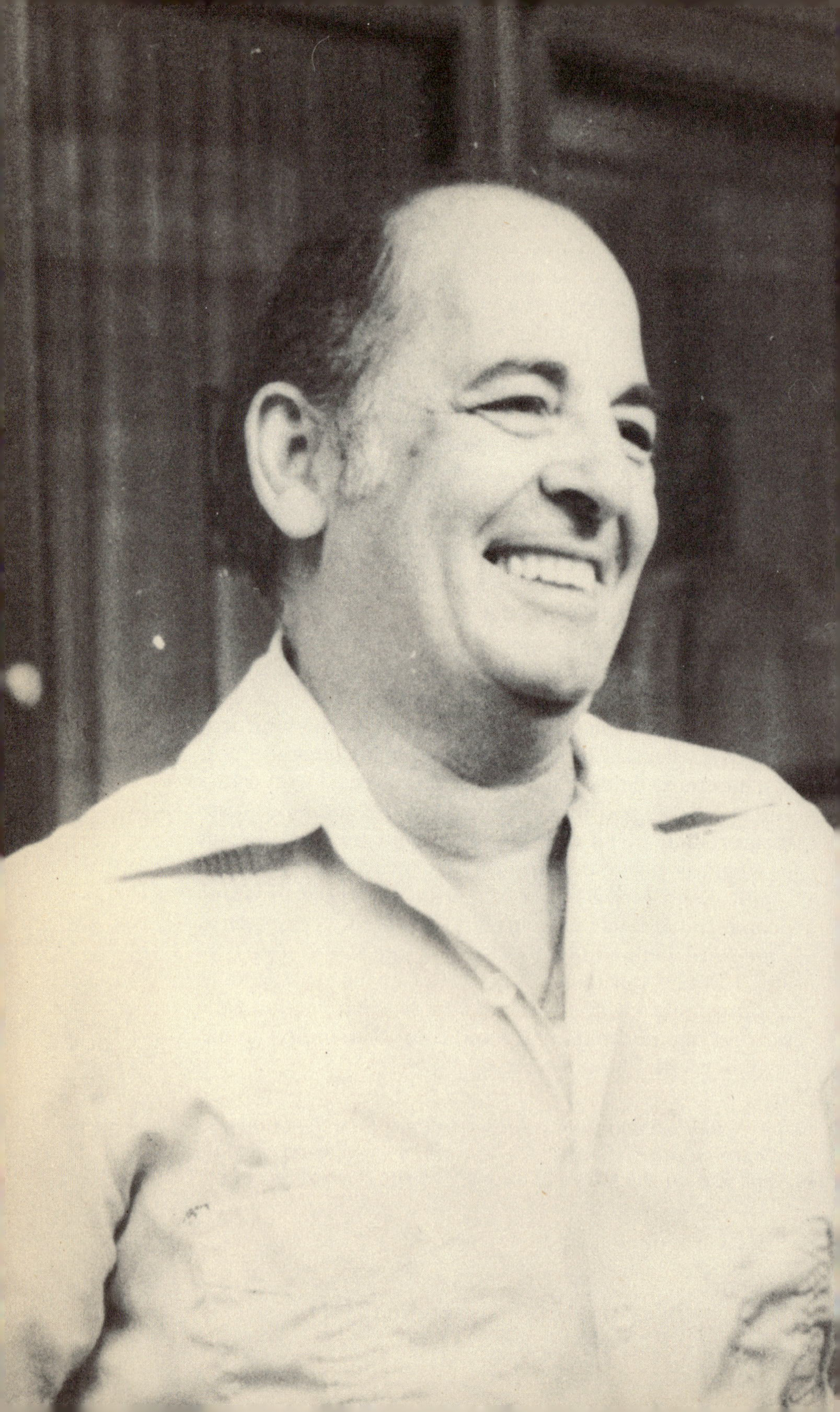

JOSEPH BUSHEME

WARDROBE MASTER
BIG RIVER ON BROADWAY

    The films *The Goodbye Girl, A Chorus Line, The Turning Point* have all tried to explore to one degree or another the life of the dancer. Dancers dedicate their lives from an early age to this brutal task that creates such beauty. Then, when they reach an age when in most professions they would expect to see economic and professional stability, suddenly they are too old to lift the leg as high, to maintain balance through an extended tableau, to turn and leap and step with the lightness and endurance of a younger person. Some turn to teaching the young. Some become bitter. Some find other ways to stay near the stage that they have loved and invested so much of their lives in.

    Joseph Busheme was a dancer. He grew up in Boston and studied at the New England Conservatory. His professional career involved many years of dancing in both Europe and America. Most of his career was with the famous Ballet Russe de Monte Carlo. It was from Mme. Pourmel, the wardrobe mistress of that legendary company, that he got the advice that helped him sustain himself when his days as a performer came to an end. She had seen him work on his own costumes. If a button needed replacing or a piece of elastic needed restitching, the young man would not bother a wardrobe person—he simply picked up needle and thread and did it himself. He often helped other dancers with their costume problems, and he seemed to have an innate understanding of how much a seam needed to be taken in or where to put a gusset. "Develop this," she said with her aristocratic European manner. "Perhaps you don't need it now, but later on . . ."

Joe took the advice to heart and watched more closely as the professional staff went about the business of mending and repairing, letting out and taking in seams, pressing and cleaning and packing and preparing the clothing that the company wore. As time went by he found himself doing more and more work with needle and thread, iron and steamer. In the early 1960s Mme. Pourmel asked him to forego dancing for one tour and go out with the company as wardrobe master. He did, and for the next several years alternated working as a dancer and as a costumer. By 1964 he had given up dancing altogether and was devoting himself to costuming on a full-time basis. A friend got him involved with the Broadway production of *High Spirits*, and he has been a professional costumer ever since. He has worked on films and television shows but has found them frustrating. A scene is filmed or taped, and the clothing for it is put away. A friend is made while the scene is being filmed, and after the scene the friend goes away. A Broadway show must, by the very nature of the work and by the close proximity in which the participants must work, become a family. Joe likes that aspect of the stage and is happy to concentrate his efforts on the plays and musicals that perform in the three dozen or so houses that constitute the Broadway theater. In 1985 designer Patricia McGourty tapped him to serve as wardrobe master of *Big*

River. He has held that post for such successes as *Applause*, *Halleluja, Baby*, *Merlin*, and the long running Bob Fosse success *Dancin'*.

From the crowded wardrobe room of the Eugene O'Neill Theatre, Joe Busheme supervises a staff of six dressers who are responsible for the care and upkeep of the 140 outfits that are worn by the twenty-three actors in *Big River*. The room is small, up two flights of stairs from the stage below. It has space for a sewing machine, an abbreviated cutting table, several racks of costumes and trays and boxes containing all the paraphernalia necessary to build and alter clothing that must be worn eight times each week. The iron and ironing board are kept on a landing just outside the door. Like the sewing machine, they are kept open and ready during each performance in case an emergency comes up. But each of the staff carries safety pins, which are the first aid of the costumer's business.

Most days Joe is in the theater by ten in the morning. He lives nearby, so the short walk from his brownstone is a bit of a blessing compared to the commuting time required of others who must fight buses and subways from farther away. There is the daily laundry to do, tights and shirts and dancewear that must be clean for every performance. There are repairs—zippers to replace, tears to mend, elastic to stitch. There is also redying, to keep the original color in the fabric. *Big River* has been running over a year now, so some of the pieces are being replaced, having been worn nearly five hundred times already. This is the daily work of the costume department before the actors ever get to the theater.

Joe Busheme is a gentle man. The discipline and order he learned as a dancer have been translated into life skills and are evident in the neatness with which his domain is organized. The trim lines of a dancer's body have rounded a bit with age, but there is still an easy grace about him as well as a soft-spoken calm born of many years of speaking near the stage where even whispers are offered with caution.

The costume master comes into the process during rehearsals. "You have to get into rehearsals to find out what the clothes have to do, what fast changes there are and how to make them work." Actually, according to Joe, that is the most important thing costumers do: make the costume work. The designer is responsible for the look of the whole show and for the individual cut and style of each costume. But the actor has to perform in that costume, and it is not unusual for an actor to feel restricted by a sleeve that is too tight or a skirt that is too full to permit the same freedom of movement planned in the rehearsal hall while the actor was wearing jeans and a shirt. The look of the costume may be perfect. The way the costume works may be another matter entirely. That is when the wardrobe master steps in with a tuck here or a release of fabric there. Dancers are usually the most concerned with the way a costume wears. They should be able to move with the same freedom they would in leotard and tights, even if they are wearing full skirts or elaborate sleeves. It is the work of Joe and his staff that makes that possible. And yet he pays homage to the designs and the designers. "They're concerned with the look of the characters. We're concerned with the actor and making sure the clothes work."

Despite that, he can tell some fascinating tales of times when the costume didn't work. In *Big River*, his current assignment, Dan Jenkins, who plays Huck Finn, wears a loose-fitting pair of pants with a single suspender. During one performance, the suspender broke. The costume staff was ready in the wings to fix the problem. It's just that Jenkins didn't come off stage for another twenty minutes. So while the safety pins were stationed backstage, he gamely carried on two scenes and a dance number with one hand free to gesture and one hand firmly at his waist.

Or take the night in Joe's first show, *High Spirits*, when one of the ghosts prepared to be lifted off her feet in a flying harness. The harness, a very secure network of leather and fiber straps, was completely invisible under the airy costume. The cable would be attached while the actress was standing on a catwalk some twenty feet above the stage floor. She would then swing out onto the stage already flying. The effect would be of a ghost suddenly appearing in midair. Unfortunately, the costume was so diaphanous that it got caught in the rigging offstage. But no one knew. When the cue came, the actress leapt off into midair. But her costume stayed firmly fixed in the wings. There she was dancing high above the stage floor wearing only—you guessed it—her flying harness.

Joe Busheme's stories of mishaps are interspersed with stories of the performers he has worked with. He remembers the young Leslie Uggams in her first starring role in *Halleluja, Baby* and the eccentric Bea Lillie in *High Spirits*. He also remembers Lauren Bacall in *Applause* and the late Anne Baxter in the same show. When Miss Baxter took over the role from Miss Bacall, one of the costumes didn't work. Miss Baxter didn't want to complain, but she was very uncomfortable in the outfit. It was Joe who went to the authorities and persuaded them to let him make a new version of the gown. Miss Baxter became a devoted friend.

It is that personal touch that has endeared him to so many of the performers he has worked with over the years. Costumers are often a combination of technician and mother, slave to the demands of the moment and friend in time of need. Because they deal so directly with the body, many actors live by the rule that "you have no secrets from God and your dresser." Actors also know that the two people you keep on good terms with are your stage manager and your costumer. Either or both can make life heaven or hell for the performer.

Joe likes to make life heaven for the people he works with. But his gentle disposition does not keep him from a realistic view of changes he has observed in over twenty years at his work. "I know a lot of kids fresh out of college with degrees in costuming. Technically, they're marvelous—they know what *should* transpire. But they don't understand what the performer is going through." Joe understands. Both from his experience on the stage and from being a friend to both stars and understudies, Joe has nurtured his love of theater with patience, expertise, and gentle, affectionate good humor. The warmth and obvious respect with which, time and again, actors stop by the costume room, stick their heads in the door, and say, "Hi, Joe," is evidence of the family feeling he instills in the people around him. He says he might retire after *Big River*. "But," he adds with a tender smile, "I don't know what else I would want to do. I love my work."

In the long-running musical *A Chorus Line*, there is a very simple line of dialogue that carries a lot of weight: "A dancer dances." It implies that it is the work that makes the artist, and when the artist isn't doing the work, he ceases to be an artist. If that is true, it is a painful truth for any performer. Yet it must also be true that, as the career of Joe Busheme shows, there is nothing wrong with picking up a new art and continuing to work in the theater you love.

Joseph Busheme (photo on page 110) in front of one of the ad posters showing the costumes he takes care of every day. (Photo by George Storey)

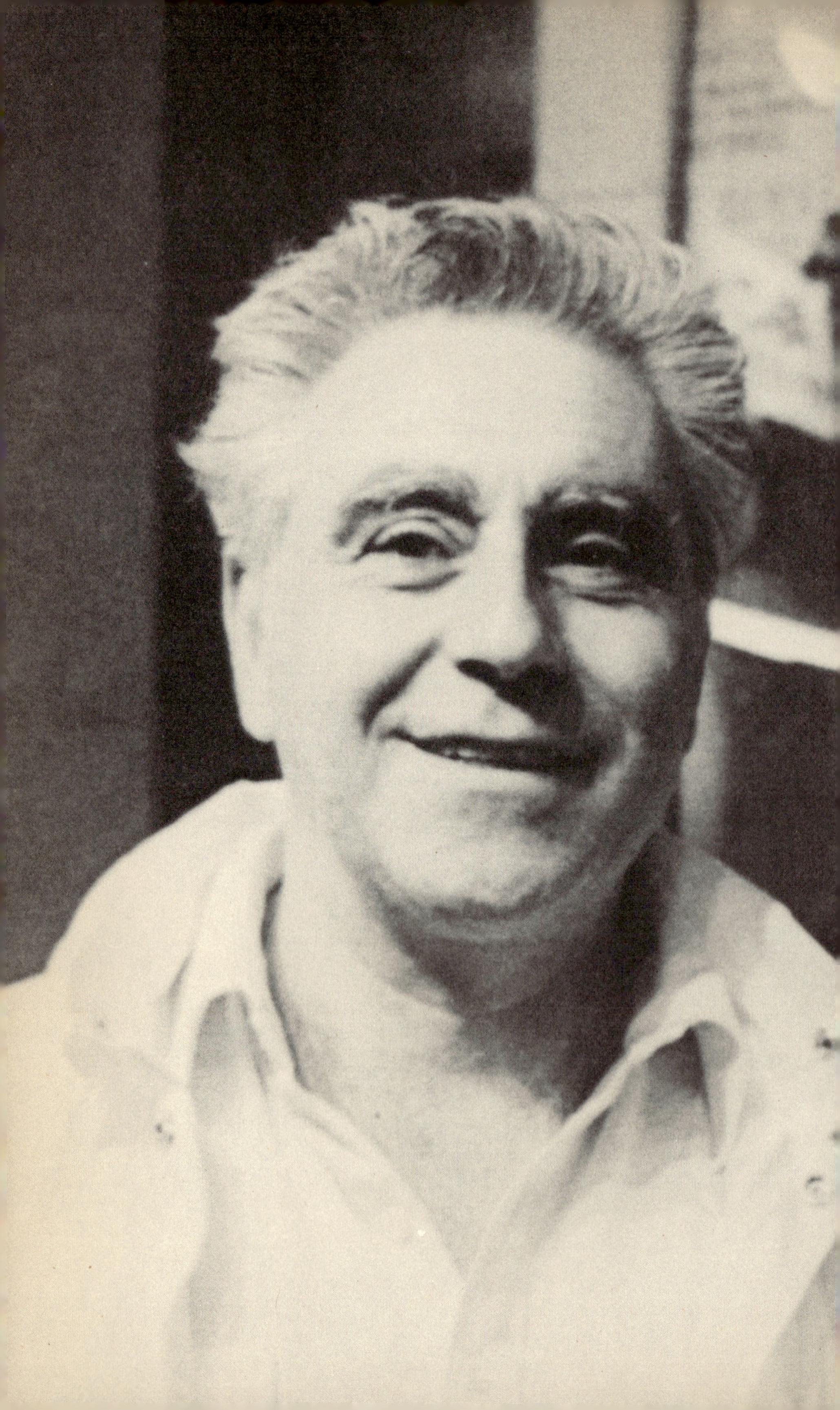

JOSEPH PATRIA
PRODUCTION CARPENTER
BIG RIVER ON BROADWAY

"The turtle is broken. Again."

The voice was calm but clearly frustrated. It came from the darkened seats of the Eugene O'Neill Theatre. It came from Heidi Landesman. Ms. Landesman was not only the set designer for *Big River*, she was also, with her husband, coproducer of the show which was about to open on Broadway. When Heidi Landesman spoke, people listened.

The word passed quickly backstage. "The turtle is broken—again." In the darkened wings Joe Patria heard it and headed for the onstage light. He arrived midstage just as Ms. Landesman came up from the audience seats. The attractive young woman stood beside the silver-haired older man. "Joe," she said, "The turtle is broken—again." And they smiled at each other. It had almost become a joke as they had worked what seemed like days on end just getting the thing to work. They both looked down at the turtle.

In front of them was a rounded turntable set in a groove in the false floor. Beneath the floor, cables carried the turntable along the groove. On top of the turntable was a platform built like a raft. The idea was for the raft to move back and forth and even turn around while both raft and turntable were being drawn across the stage by the hidden cables. With fog all around and appropriate lighting the raft was to look as if it were floating on the Mississippi. It was a spectacular effect. Except now the turtle was broken.

Joe Patria examined the groove and the raft and made a few suggestions. If the groove could be reshaped in this direction a bit and the raft placed just here, maybe . . . Joe is accustomed to making such suggestions. He has been working with scenery for more than thirty years. But he has been around show business all his life.

Joe's father was with the circus. He traveled while his family lived in Connecticut. Later he worked in movie theaters, and when Joe got old enough, he would sometimes help his father. But Joe had plans. He wanted to be a teacher. The hours appealed to him. The vacations were generous, and the life was predictable. Teaching seemed to be a nice orderly way to make a living.

All that changed in 1955 when down the road at Stratford, Connecticut, the American Shakespeare Festival opened. They were hiring stagehands, and for Joe it seemed like an easy way to spend the summer. Now, more than thirty years later, Joe Patria is still on the staff.

In 1955 the regional theater movement in America was in its infancy. A few major cities had touring houses, but there were no more than a handful of professional companies outside New York. Many major stars were excited about the prospect of a serious professional theater dedicated to Shakespeare and agreed to become part of the Stratford Company. Among them was Katherine Hepburn.

During that first season Joe found himself captivated by the people and the work of live theater. This was not like changing a movie marquee or adjusting a screen. This was being part of a living performance with people who took their work very seriously. It was also a lot of fun. Today Joe Patria says, "The secret of this business is that you work eighty hours a week and you go home and the next morning you're excited about going to work again."

Part of Joe's work during that first season at Stratford was to help Miss Hepburn up a ladder. The show was *Antony and Cleopatra*. Miss Hepburn was to make her entrance on top of a large Egyptian sphinx. Joe was to help her get up there.

Joe arrived in his position backstage for the first time, and so did Miss Hepburn. As the cue for her entrance grew closer, the two nodded to each other and turned to the ladder. She started to step up, and Joe was right beside her. Unfortunately, she was wearing a costume with yards of flowing fabric. Joe discovered that he was standing on her costume. He stepped away to release the skirt, but she started to falter, and he stepped in again only to find that he was again standing on her dress and she was trapped. Finally Joe just moved away altogether, and the notoriously independent Miss Hepburn ascended the stairs on her own. At intermission Joe was not surprised to hear the voice over the intercom say, "Joe Patria—to Miss Hepburn's dressing room—immediately!" He knocked on the door gently, almost hoping she would not notice. But her distinctive voice said, "Come in," and he opened the door with caution. "You wanted to see me?" She turned and looked at him for a moment. Then, with the same hushed tone she had sometimes used on screen with Cary Grant and James Stewart and Spencer Tracy, she said, "Joe, just don't *help* me anymore, please."

When Stratford was not performing, Joe began to take work with tours and, eventually, with New York shows. Working his way up, he has become one of a small group of master stagehands in the business. The job title is production carpenter. But the work involves much more than hammer and nails. Joe knows more about engineering than many bridge builders. He has worked with metals and plastics and fabrics and wood, as well as with all the many kinds of machines used to operate shows like the James Earl Jones *Othello, The Tap Dance Kid,* and the long-running *Annie.* Such work has brought him into contact with all styles of designwork creating any kind of location that can be imagined. "We (meaning the theater) can fake everything but the floor," says Joe.

For *Big River,* Joe supervises a crew of sixteen who handle both the scenery that rides on the stage itself and the drops that hang above the stage. They are operated from the "fly floor" some twenty feet above the stage. This crew also takes care of all the props the actors carry. Because the set is elaborate and the stage is relatively small, some whole platforms must be "flown" into the air in odd corners of the stage when they are not in use. Other pieces are set up in the cable grooves in the floor and then are operated by electrical winch.

The work and the people who do it keep Joe happy. Only once during his adult life has he worked outside the theater. He thought more regular hours and weekends off might be better for his family. His two sons were still at home then. He was offered a position with the City of Bridgeport (Connecticut), as Director of Housing Site Development. But the "civilian" world was not the place for Joe. "Can you imagine seventeen people having a meeting to decide when to have the next meeting? In the theater you decide to make a change at midnight, and by 1:00 the next afternoon when the actors come in, it's all done."

But it was more than the inefficiency of government that bothered Joe. There is a sly smile playing across his face as he points out the irony that carried him back to the stage after only a year and a half in what many people think of as the "real" world. "Government is make-believe make-believe. You plan and plan and budget and budget. But the planning and the budgeting become more important than the thing you're there to do. The curtain never goes up. It's never opening night. Theater is the *real* world of make-believe." He is wisely realistic about the limitations of his trade: "We in the technical department can help a show be better, but we can't make a show. No show was ever a success if the scenery was good and the actors were bad." At the same time he is clear about what it is he does and why he does it. "Theater is really make-believe, and everybody knows it. And we do it because that's our job—to make believe. What's wrong with that?"

Joe Patria's smile (see photo on page 118) is a key to understanding his enjoyment of every day's work as production carpenter for Big River and as technical director for The American Shakespeare Festival. (Photo by George Storey)

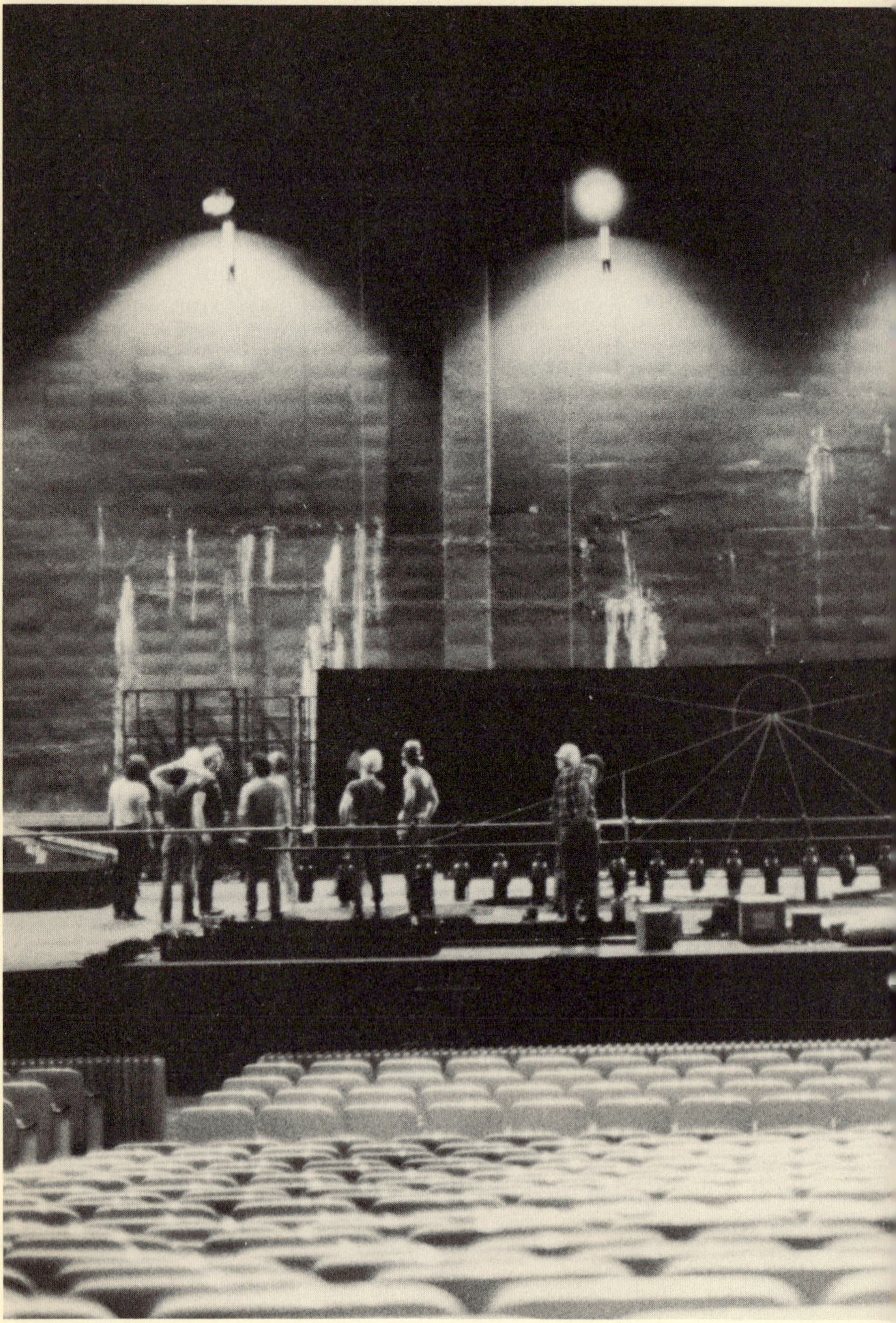

RUNNING THE PERFORMANCE 125

"Take-in" day, the day the set moves into the theater, is long and exhausting for every one of the dozens of people involved.

126   BEHIND THE SCENES

Commercial productions hire crews of dozens of extra hands to move in the tons of equipment which provide the environment for the play.

Hundreds of instruments are required to light a major production. Each ranges in power from 500 watts to 1500 watts.

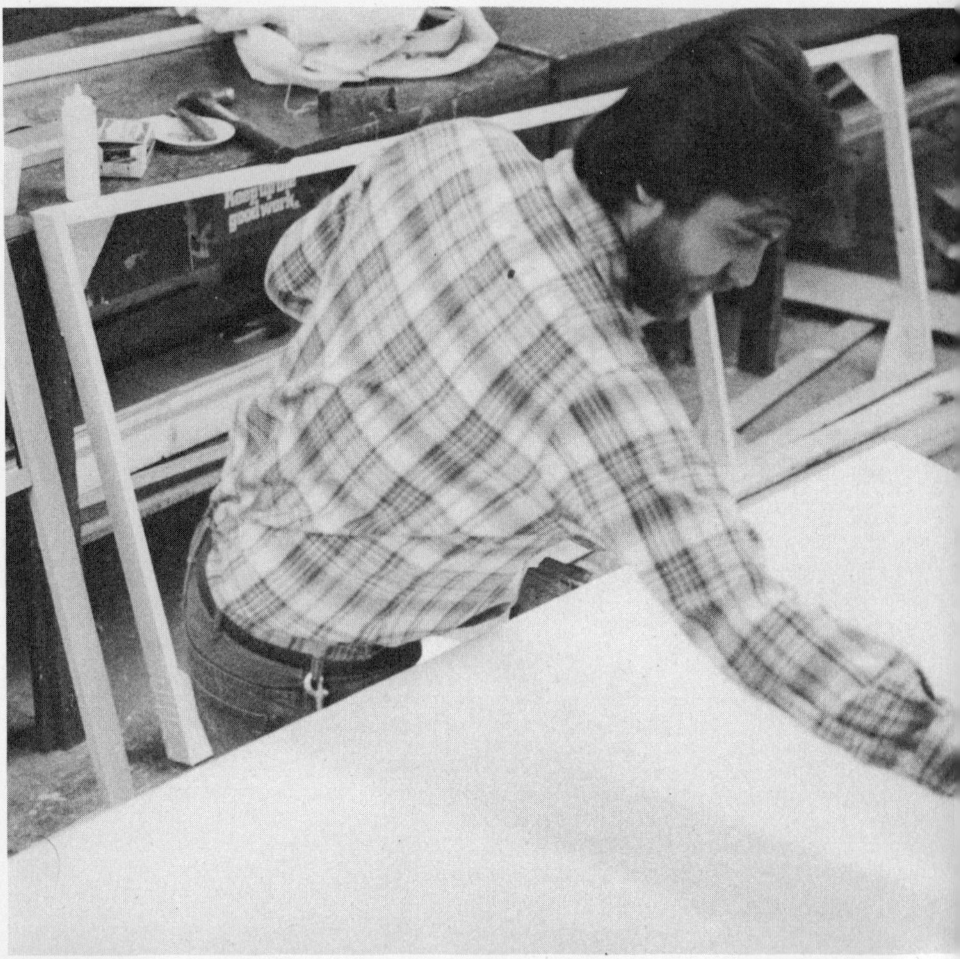

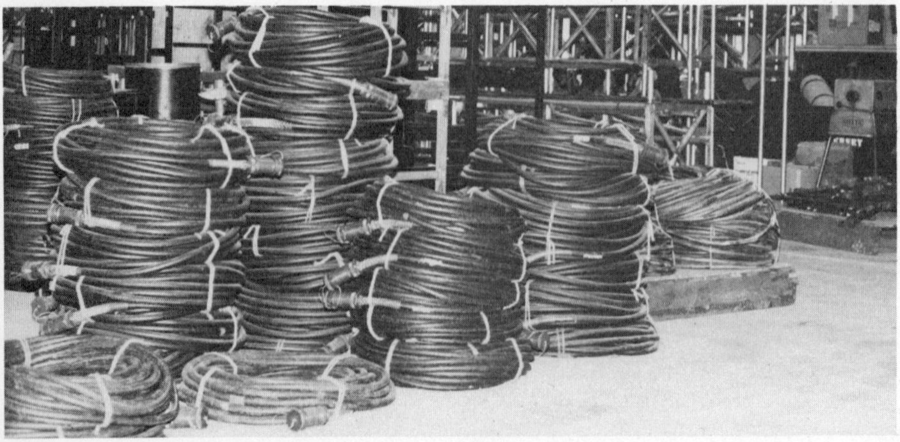

No matter how carefully a set has been planned, there are frequently scenic pieces that cannot be built until the set is in place on stage in the theater. Then small units can be added which put the final touches on the look of the show, and it is not unusual for designers and technicians to work round the clock during set-up week in order to get a show ready to open.

Miles of cable are used to connect these instruments to the control board which fades them on and off.

The actors and their costumes are ready. Costumes range from traditional garments to specialty items made up of painted rags and chains. (Pictured are the author as Marley's Ghost and Don Christopher as Scrooge in the TheatreVirginia production of A Christmas Carol.)

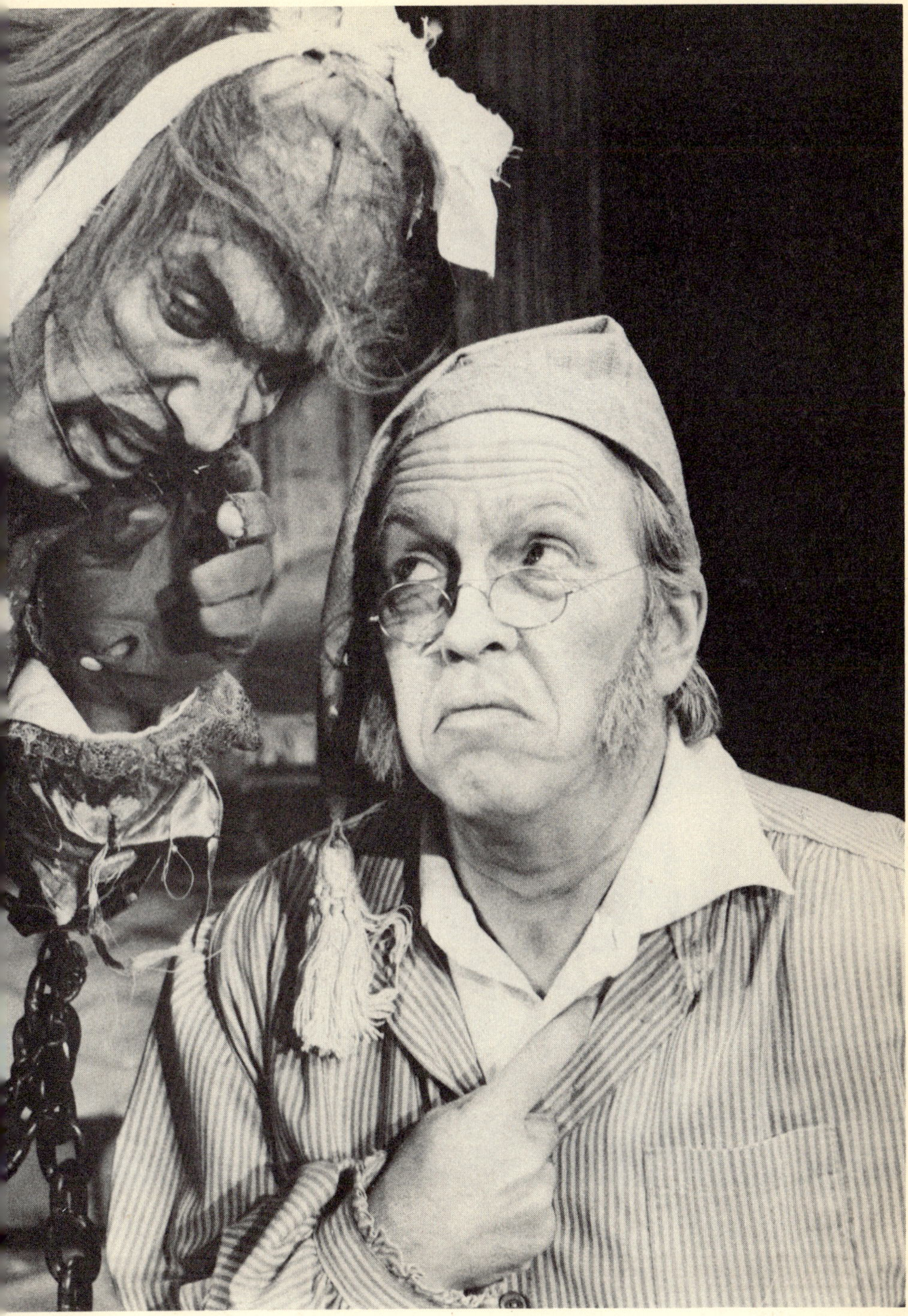

132 BEHIND THE SCENES

These technicians are working on the TheatreVirginia production of The Fourposter. The play has only two *characters, but takes a crew of seven to make the rapid changes of props and set decorations.*

134 BEHIND THE SCENES

Meanwhile, the promotion and press people have been doing their job. An advertising logo has been adopted which will plant the image of the play firmly in the public mind.

RUNNING THE PERFORMANCE 135

Part of the promotion effort is the distribution of tickets to outlets other than the box office. Sometimes blocks of tickets are given to hospitals and other organizations. Sometimes cut-price tickets are offered at places like this discount ticket center in Times Square where half-price tickets for many Broadway shows can be purchased in the hours just before a performance. (See Glossary—TKTS)

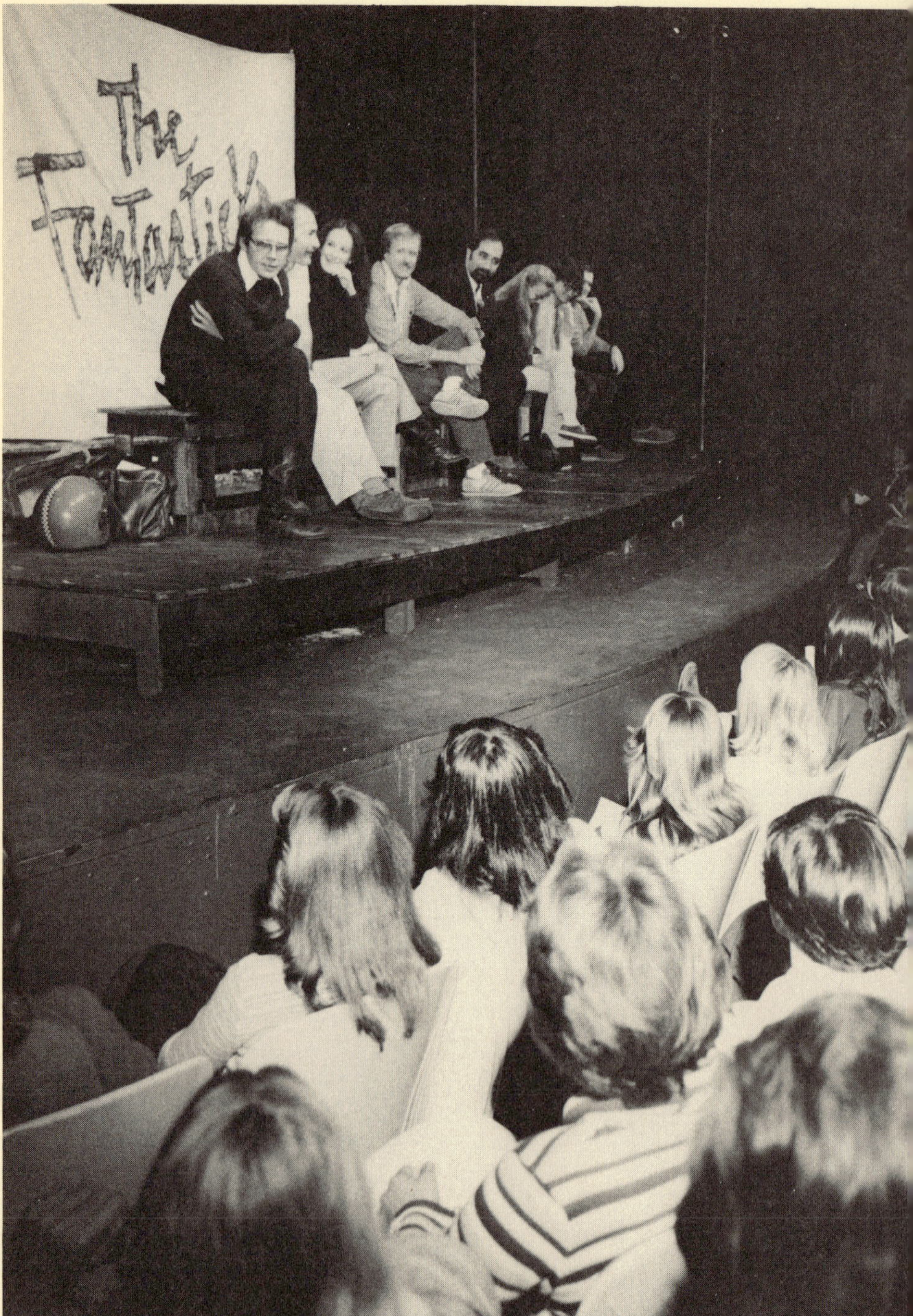
The Fantasticks

RUNNING THE PERFORMANCE   137

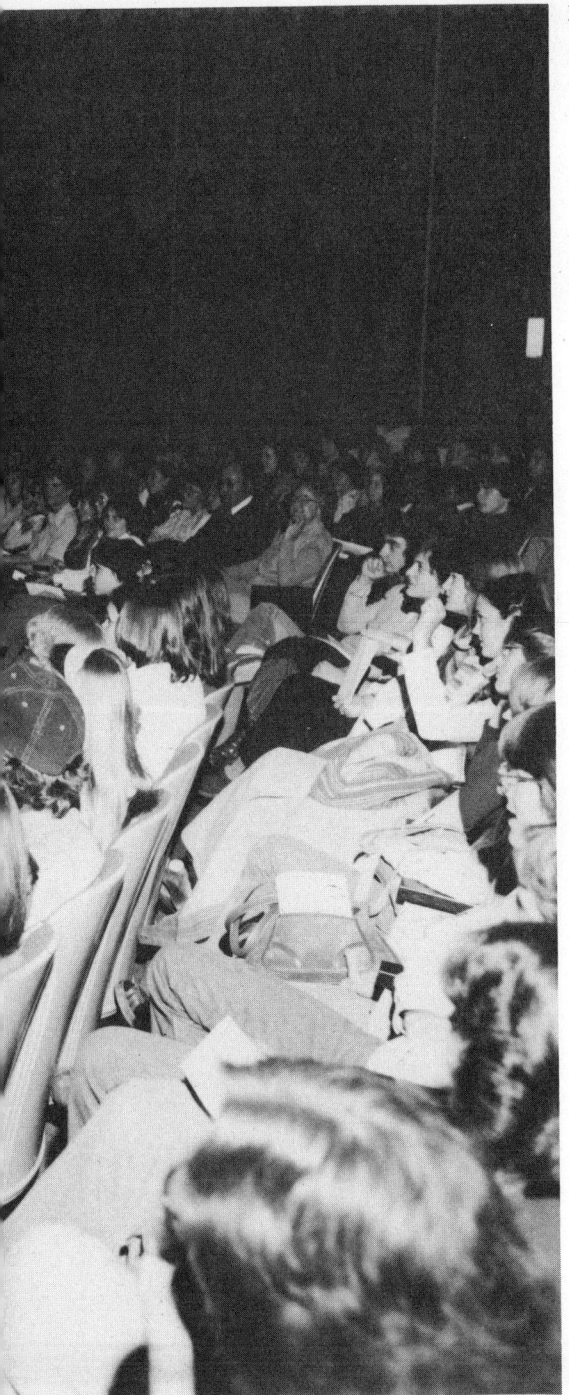

Sometimes press representatives set up interviews with cast and crew for student groups. This session at TheatreVirginia gave a school group a chance to talk with the cast of The Fantasticks.

Around the country hundreds of people crowd into professional regional and community theaters while . . .

. . . in New York thousands of patrons arrive by subway, bus, taxi and private car to enjoy the wonder of theater.

Behind the scenes, dozens of professional performers and technicians work and rehearse and prepare so that they can be ready to entertain the audience when the curtain goes up.

(Photo Credits: 1, 2, 3, 4, courtesy of Vanco Stage Lighting; 5, 6, 8, 10, 13, courtesy of TheatreVirginia; 7, 9, 11, 12, from the author's collection.)

APPENDIX A

UNIONS

Regional theaters usually deal with only one or two unions. In most cases Actors' Equity Association represents actors in a regional theater, and, if the theater is large or houses tours, the stagehands may be members of a local of IATSE (International Alliance of Theatrical Stage Employees).* New York, on the other hand, has separate unions that represent almost every aspect of theatrical production. Some will provide information sheets on the union's activities. If you are interested in a particular kind of work, you may wish to write for such an information sheet.

Actors' Equity Association (Equity or AEA)
165 West 46th Street
New York, New York 10036
Represents actors and stage managers.

American Federation of Musicians
1500 Broadway
New York, New York 10036
Represents musicians, arrangers, orchestrators, copyists, etc.

Association for Theatre Press Agents and Managers (ATPAM)
268 West 47th Street
New York, New York 10036
Represents press agents, company managers, and house managers.

Dramatists Guild
234 West 44th Street
New York, New York 10036
Represents playwrights, composers, and lyricists.

*International Alliance of Theatrical Stage Employees and Moving Picture Machine Operators of the United States and Canada (IATSE or IA)
1515 Broadway
New York, New York 10036
IATSE represents most of the theatrical technicians through locals that concentrate on specific crafts. Local 1 is the New York organization of stage carpenters, property persons, and electricians. Local 751 represents box-office personnel. Local 764 represents theatrical wardrobe attendants. Each of these locals has its own office and staff. The main office can provide more information about the union and its activities.

Society of Stage Directors and Choreographers (SSDC)
1501 Broadway
New York, New York 10036

United Scenic Artists
1540 Broadway
New York, New York 10036
Represents designers and scenic artists.

SERVICE ORGANIZATIONS

Each of these organizations has a specific service area. Some have student memberships. Write for more information.

Alliance of Resident Theatres/New York
325 Spring Street
New York, New York 10013
Service organization for not-for-profit New York theaters.

Black Theatre Alliance
410 West 42nd Street
New York, New York 10019

Foundation for the Extension and Development of the American Professional Theatre (FEDAPT)
165 West 46th Street
New York, New York 10036
Consulting organization for theater administration.

Theatre Communications Group
355 Lexington Avenue
New York, New York 10017
Service organization for not-for-profit regional theaters.

U.S. Institute for Theatre Technology (USITT)
330 West 42nd Street
New York, New York 10036

APPENDIX B

RELATED READING

There are a number of books about how to produce theater. The books listed here are particularly helpful in looking at the employment situation.

Folke, Ann, and Richard Harden. *Opportunities in Theatrical Design and Production.* Lincolnwood, Illinois: National Textbook Company, 1985.

Katz, Judith A. *The Business of Show Business.* New York: Barnes & Noble, 1981.

Greenburg, Jan. *Theatre Careers: A Comprehensive Guide to Non-Acting Careers in the Theatre.* New York: Holt, Rinehart and Winston, 1983.

Gruver, Bert. *Stage Manager's Handbook.* Revised Edition. New York: Drama Book Publishers, 1972.

Tompkins, Dorothy Lee. *Handbook for Theatrical Apprentices, A Practical Guide for All Phases of Theatre.* New York: Samuel French, 1962.

GLOSSARY

AGENT An agent represents actors, writers, and directors by submitting them for consideration for jobs, negotiating contracts, and sorting out conflicts between jobs. Agents are franchised by the unions and take a percentage commission for their work.

AFTRA The American Federation of Television and Radio Artists is the actors' union that oversees all live and videotaped broadcasting.

APPRENTICE An apprentice is a beginner working to become a union member. Many of the theatrical unions have apprenticeship programs. The most familiar is through Actors' Equity. Equity apprentices, sometimes called interns, help out backstage, build scenery and costumes, usher, and sometimes play small roles in regional and summer companies. While off-Broadway theaters sometimes use apprentices, Broadway theaters are not allowed to employ apprentice performers.

BACKER A backer is anyone who invests money in a production. Each commercial production is set up as an independent corporation, and the backers, sometimes called "angels," are the stockholders.

CALL Call refers to any appointment at a specific time. There are rehearsal calls, costume calls for fittings, photo calls for picture taking, work calls for technical crews, etc.

CALL BOARD The call board is the official bulletin board where schedules, information, notices, messages, etc., are posted. Usually mounted near the stage door to the theater, the call board is also where actors and technicians sign in each time they report to the theater.

CARD A union membership card is used to identify union members at interviews, auditions, and union activities. In New York some merchants will give discounts on goods and services upon presentation of a union card.

CHOREOGRAPHER Dances and complex movement sequences like fight scenes are designed by a choreographer.

CONTRACT A contract is a legal document that states the terms of an agreement. Theater contracts include all the standard work rules of a particular union and any other provisions either the producer or the worker negotiates. Each of the major unions sets a standard contract with the association of producers. Individual contracts then refer to that base contract.

CONVERSION When a production moves from one size theater to another (e.g., off Broadway to Broadway) it converts to the new contract rules for that theater.

COSTUMES Anything an actor wears onstage is considered a costume, whether it is a period garment or a T-shirt and jeans.

DRESS Dress is slang for "dress rehearsal," at which costumes and makeup and all technical effects are tried out.

DUES Dues are payments to the union by the worker. Some unions charge a fixed amount. Others charge a percentage of wages. Some charge both.

FLY FLOOR All hanging scenery is operated by ropes that are controlled from a platform called the fly floor. The ropes pass through pulleys in a grid above the stage. They then pass to the offstage position and are "counterweighted" with sandbags or lead blocks that allow the "fly man" to raise and lower the scenery with minimal effort.

FOLLOWSPOT The strong clear light that follows a performer around the stage is called a followspot. Followspots are operated individually. Some followspots contain large incandescent lamps, and some contain electric arc lights.

HALF HOUR Half hour is a call thirty minutes before curtain time. All members of the company are supposed to be in the theater by half hour.

INITIATION FEE A payment to the union at the time a worker joins is called an initiation fee. These fees range from $500 in some unions to several thousand in others.

LOCAL Unions are organized to represent the needs of different kinds of workers. The organization of a particular union in a particular city is called the local. Thus, for stagehands, Local 1 in New York sets up rules and contracts for the membership of that local. But those rules do not apply to stagehands in another city who have their own local.

MANAGEMENT The owners and operators of a production or theater company are known collectively as manage ment. This is a union term and is meant to define the differences between the people who perform or provide a service (actors, stagehands, directors, designers, etc.) and those who hire them (producers, general managers, casting directors, etc.).

MATINEE An afternoon performance is called a matinee.

MINIMUM A minimum is the lowest salary the union will allow a member to be paid in a particular theater. Workers can negotiate salaries higher than the minimum if their reputations and abilities warrant such increases.

NOT-FOR-PROFIT Theaters and other organizations which are set up for the public good and from which no individual makes a personal profit are granted not-for-profit (NPO or nonprofit organization) status by U.S. tax laws. These companies can then solicit grants and moneys from foundations and individuals and carry a greater operating loss than investment-based businesses.

OPTION A producer will sometimes take an option on a script. This means that he pays the writer to withhold permission from other producers to perform the script until the optioning producer has decided whether or not to mount a production.

PREVIEW Many productions give several public or private performances before the official opening of a show so that actors and directors can see how the show works in front of an audience and make changes, if necessary, before the critics see the production on opening night.

REGIONAL THEATER Beginning in the mid-1950s, professional theaters began appearing all over the country. There had always been summer operations in vacation areas, but these new theaters were year-round operations with full-time professional staffs, and they planned repertories of classical drama as well as contemporary comedy. At the same time, dinner theaters, which provided a meal and a show under the same roof, began to appear. For the first time, in the late 1960s, there was more professional work outside New York than in Broadway and off-Broadway shows. Today there are several hundred regional theaters all over America. They provide employment opportunities for actors and technicians, as well as starting places for theater administrators.

REHEARSAL The work sessions at which the actors and director arrange movement (blocking) and practice performing the play are called rehearsals. Technicians also rehearse with and without actors in order to work out complex scenery shifts and lighting effects.

STAR A star is anyone whose name is likely to attract people to the theater.

STOCK The term "stock" comes from a time when most plays had a standard set of characters. Touring stock companies were made up of a leading man and leading lady, a young leading couple, and character men and women. In stock companies today, one or two actors will play all the leading parts, and other roles will be taken by character people. Apprentices may then get to play any parts that are left over.

STRIKE To strike is to remove something. A prop may be struck, or an entire set may be removed from the stage or from the theater. A director may say, "Strike the candles from that table," meaning take the candles away. A stage manager may say, "Strike the Act I set, and set up for Act II," meaning remove one set and set up another. When a play closes, the entire set is "struck," or removed from the theater.

TECH Technical rehearsals are for the people who run the lights and sound and move scenery and props. Actors walk through their movements and say the lines that cue the effects. That way the technicians can see exactly how long they have to run their various cues.

THEATRE Most people involved in theater spell the word with an "re" ending instead of the American standard "er." This is out of respect for the Greek origin of the term *theatron*, which was first translated as "theatre."

TRADES On Wednesday and Thursday of each week, several newspapers are issued in New York that have casting news and items about the theater and media trades. These trade papers are usually spoken of as "the trades."

TRYOUT Before a play opens in New York, a producer will often set up short runs in cities such as Boston, Philadelphia, or Washington so that the piece can be "tried out" in front of audiences. Often changes are made in the play or in scenery or costumes based on these performances.

UPTOWN/DOWNTOWN Most of the Broadway theaters are located around Times Square in New York. This is considered "uptown," since most of the off-Broadway theaters are in Greenwich Village, which is "downtown." Ironically some off-Broadway theaters are farther uptown than the Broadway theaters. When *Hurlyburly* opened at a theater on Seventy-seventh Street, it was considered off Broadway. When it moved to a Broadway theater on Forty-seventh Street (downtown), it was reported to be moving "uptown."

INDEX

Abrams, Anne, 66–68
Actors, xv, xviii, 91; and costumers, 115–116; rewards of, xx
Actors' Equity Association, 149, 145
Actors' Theatre of Louisville, 11
Adler, Steven, 97
Advertisement, 91
Advertising agencies, xvii, 47
Advertising campaigns, 33–34
AFTRA (American Federation of Television and Radio Artists), 145
Agent, 145
Alliance of Resident Theatres/New York, 141
American Federation of Musicians, 139
American Repertory Theatre (Cambridge, Mass.), 92
American Shakespeare Festival, 120–121
Andrews, Julie, 27
Annie (play), 122
Anthony and Cleopatra (play), 121
Applause (play), 113, 115

Apprentice, 145
Arena Stage (Washington), 51
Art form: theater as, xix
Art Institute of Chicago, 58
Artistic director: T. Burgler, 48–55
Artistic standards, xix, 23–24, 50
Arts management, xix
Association of Theatre Press Agents and Managers (ATPAM), 68, 140
Astor Place Theatre, 32, 33
Audience, 47
Audition process, 46–47

Bacall, Lauren, 115
Backer, 145
Ballet Russe de Monte Carlo, 111–112
Baxter, Anne, 115
Bernhardt, Sarah, xx
Big Deal (play), 60–61, 63–64, 68–69, 70–71
Big River (play), 92, 95, 97, 98, 103, 104, 106, 107, 108, 109, 112–113, 114–115, 116, 122
Black Theatre Alliance, 141

Blacks, The (play), 60
Bloomgarden, Kermit, 8–9
Bolt, Gigi, 9
Bolt, Jonathan, 5–14
Bolt, Julie, 9
Box-office clerks, xx, 91
Brandeis University, 60–61
Breakfast with Les and Bess (play), 24
Brighton Beach Memoirs (play), 106
Broadway, xix, 60, 65, 67, 97, 109; magic of, 70–71
Broadway theater, 23, 24, 32, 112
Broadway theaters, 108
Budget, 54
Burgler, Terry, 48–55
Burton, Richard, 68
Busheme, Joseph, 110–116
Business: theater as, xix
Business managers, xvi
Business side of producing, 3
Business training, xix

Cabaret (play), 57, 60
Call, 146
Call board, 146
Cane, Marianne, 94–100
Card, 146
Career(s): accident, chance in, 3, 57–58; reading list for, 143
Carpenter(s), 104, 106–107; J. Patria, 118–123
Casting, 46–47
Cats (play), 66, 68
Chapin, Harry, 24
Characters, 1, 2
Chicago (play), 57
Choreographer, 146
Chorus Line, A (film), 111
Chorus Line, A (play), 46, 116
Circle in the Square, 59–60

Circle Repertory Company (New York City), 10, 11
Cleveland Playhouse, 9
Community theater, 109
Company manager, xvii, 92; duties of, 33
Computerized equipment, 104, 106
Contracts, 22, 29, 33; defined, 146
Conversion, 146
Copeland, Carolyn Rossi, 16–25
Copeland, Jamie, 24
Copperfield, David, 32
Costs, xviii
Costume design, 114
Costume designers: P. Zipprodt, 56–61
Costumers, 112–116
Costumes, xix, 45–46, 91, 114–115, 146
Cotton Patch Gospel (play), 24
Craft: theater as, xix
Creative team, xviii
Crew (the), xvi–xvii
Critics, 32, 69, 70, 71
Curse of the Aching Heart, The (play), 29
Custodians, 91

Dalrymple, Jean, xx
Dames at Sea (play), 24
Dancers, 111, 114, 116
Dancin' (play), 113
Derricks, Cleavant, 64, 68
Designers, xviii, 45–46, 108
Details, 29
Development officers, xix
Devine, Loretta, 64, 68
Dialogue, 1
Dinner theater, 53
Director(s), xx, 45, 108; functions of, xviii, 54; selection of actors, 46–47
Director's Guild of America, 29–30

Dodger Productions, 106–107
Dorothy Olim Associates, 29, 33, 34–35
Dramatists Guild, 57, 140
Dress, 146
Dressers, xx. *See also* Costumers
Drew, Ellen, xx
Drury Lane, 27
Dues, 147
Dunaway, Faye, 29

Education specialists, xix
Ego, xviii
Electricians: K. Elrod, 102–109
Electricity, 104, 105
Electronics, xix
Elliot Feld Company, 35
Elmer, George, 25–35
Elmer, Jason, 30–31, 35
Elmer, Luico, 35
Elmer, Rosanne, 30–31, 35
Elon College, 7
Elrod, Keith, 102–109
"Entertainment Tonight," 69
Eugene O'Neill Theatre, 95, 104, 113, 119
Experience, 33, 59; varied, 51–52
Experiment: theater as, xix
Eye and the Hands of God (play), 9

Fashion Institute of Technology, 58–59, 60
Fehribach, Robert, 106, 107
Fiddler on the Roof (play), 57, 60
Fielder, Chris, 96–97, 99
Film(s), 50
Financing, xviii–xix, 3, 34
Fink, Bert, 62–71
First Lady (play), 10
Fly floor, 122, 147
Followspot, 147

Fosse, Bob, 64, 71, 113
Foundation for the Extension and Development of the American Professional Theatre (FEDAPT), 141
Fred Nathan Company, 68
Friedman, Robert, 11, 12
Front-office work, xix, 32, 33
Front-of-the-house staff, 92

General manager(s), 3, 92; duties of, xvii, 33–34; G. Elmer, 26–35
Godspell (play), 20
Goodbye Girl, The (film), 111
Graduate, The (film), 57
Guest spots, 68–69

Half hour, 147
Halleluja, Baby (play), 113, 115
"Hands Across America," 57
Harrison, Rex, 27, 32
Hartenstein, Frank, 97
Hayes, Helen, 57
Hedda Gabler (play), 52
Hepburn, Katherine, 32, 120, 121
High Spirits (play), 112, 115
Historians (dramaturges), xix
Hodges, Raymond, 28
Hoffman, Dustin, 64
Hollins College, 19
House managers, 91
Huckleberry Finn (Twain), 92, 97
Hughes, Barnard, 11
Humana Festival, 11

Idealism, 35
Initiation fee, 147
Institution: theater as, xix
International Alliance of Theatrical Stage Employees and Moving Picture Motion Operators of the United States (IATSE), 107, 139, 141
Investors, 3

Jacques Brel Is Alive and Well and Living in Paris (play), 30–31
Jenkins, Dan, 99, 114–115
Jones, James Earl, 122
Jones, Neal, 97

Klekas, Maggie, 21–22

LaBelle, Patti, 64
La Jolla Playhouse (San Diego, Calif.), 96, 97
Lambs Club (New York City), 18, 20
Lamb's Downstairs, 24
Lamb's Theatre (New York City), 17–18, 23–24, 25
Lamb's Theatre Company, 17–18
Landesman, Heidi, 107, 119
Landesman, Rocco, 92
Lansbury, Angela, 57
Lash, Joseph P., 6
Lazy Susan Dinner Theater, 53
Lesseps, Ferdinand de, 11
Light board, 104
Lighting cues, 108
Lighting designer(s), 107
Lighting equipment, xix, 93, 107–108
Lillie, Bea, 115
Literary devices, 2
Literary managers, xix
Local, 147
Look Homeward Angel (play), 8
Love of work, 100, 116, 121

McAnuff, Des, 97, 107
McGourty, Patricia, 112
Machinery (stage), 103, 104, 119–120, 122
Management, 147–148
Manhattan Church of the Nazarene, 18, 20, 23
Manhattan Theatre Club, 96–97

Materials management, xix
Matinee, 148
Maybe I'm Doing It Wrong (play), 29, 97
Media, 69
Merlin (play), 113
Miller, Arthur, 7
Miller, Roger, 92
Minimum, 148
Moseby Dinner Theater, 53
Mulhare, Edward, 27
My Fair Lady (play), 27–28, 32

Noncommercial theater, 53
Nathan, Fred, 64, 66, 67–68, 70, 71
New England Conservatory, 111
New York City Ballet, 58
New York University, 60
Newman, Randy, 29, 97
Nixon, Richard, 18
Noises Off (play), 68
Noncommercial professional theater, xviii–xix
Not-for-profit, 148
Not-for-profit theaters, xix; financing productions in, 3

Off-Broadway, 97
O'Neill Center (New York City), 10
Opening night, 69–70
Opening-night parties, 32, 63–64, 70
Option, 148
Option fee, 3
Othello (play), 122
Outreach directors, xix

Painting Churches (play), 24
Paranoia, xviii
Passion (play), 7
Patria, Joseph, 118–123
Penn and Teller, 57

Performance(s), 91–92
Perkins, Anthony, 8
Phoenix Theater, 60
Photographs, 22, 47, 64, 69
Pippin (play), 57, 65
Plays, 2. *See also* Script(s)
Playwrights. *See* Writers (playwrights)
Plaza Suite (play), 57
Potting Shed, The (play), 59
Pourmel, Mme., 111–112
Press agents, xvii, 47; B. Fink, 62–71; work of, 69–70
Press coverage, 70
Press releases, 22, 32, 33, 69
Preview, 148
Prince, Hal, 60
Prine, Andrew, 8, 9
Princeton University, 49, 50
Private Lives (play), 68
Producers, xx, 2–3; C. R. Copeland, 16–25; function of, xvii, 25; responsibilities of, 34
Production: creation of, 45–47
Production budgets, 22, 33
Professionalism, xvii, 29, 106
Profits/losses, 34
Programs, xv–xvi, 69
Props, 91, 122

Quinn, Anthony, 78

Reagan, Nancy, 5, 7
Regional repertory companies, 53
Regional theater, xix, 120, 139; defined, 148–149
Rehearsals, 47, 97–98, 114; defined, 149; technical, 149–150; understudy, 96
Reichold Center for the Performing Arts, 20, 21–23

Research, 11
Reviews, reviewing, 64, 65–66, 69, 70–71
Riddell, Richard, 107, 109
Robbins, Jerome, 60
Rodino, Peter, 18–19
Romantic Comedy (play), 32
Roosevelt, Eleanor, 5, 6, 7, 10
Roosevelt, Theodore, 10
Rosenthal, Jean, xx
Royalties, 2

St. Thomas, V.I., 19, 20–21
Scenery, xix, 47–48, 91, 103, 104, 108, 119–120, 122
Script(s), 2–3, 45, 54; selection for production, 25, 34
Season, 54
Self-confidence, xviii
Service organizations, 141
Set designer, xviii
1776 (film), 57
1776 (play), 65
Situations, 1, 2
Society of Stage Directors and Choreographers (SSDC), 140
Solomon's Child (play), 29
Sound, xix
Sound technicians, xvi, 104–105
Souvenir program, 69
Staff, 54, 92
Staffing, xix
Stage hands, xx
Stage manager(s), xvi, 92, 104, 108; M. Cane, 94–100; function of, 97–99
Stage West (Springfield, Mass.), 51, 52
Star, 149
Statistical records, 33
Stock, 149
Strike, 149

156 BEHIND THE SCENES

Sunday in the Park with George (play), 68
SUNY-Purchase, 65–66
Supervising technical positions, 106–107
Sweet Charity (play), 58

Tap Dance Kid, The (play), 122
Tavern on the Green, 63–64, 70
Taylor, Elizabeth, 68
Tech (defined), 149–150
Technicians, xvi–xvii, 91–92, 104–105, 106–107, 140
Technology, xviii, xix
Teddy (play), 8, 9
Theater, 50–51, 55, 95–96, 123; defined, 150; facets of, xix; specialized positions in, xix
Theater manager, 92
Theater selection, 33–34
Theatre Communications Group, 141
TheatreVirginia, 49
Theatreworks USA, 10
Theatrical devices, 2
Threads (play), 9, 10, 13
To Culebra (play), 11–12
"Today Show," 68–69
Tomlin, Lily, 57
Tony awards, 57, 58, 109
Trades, 150
Tryout, 150
Tulane University, 19
Turning Point, The (play), 111
Twain, Mark: *Huckleberry Finn*, 92, 97

UCLA, 96
Uggams, Leslie, 115
Understudies, 96, 98

Union regulations, 29, 33
Unions, 3, 139–140; design, 59
United Scenic Artists, 140
U.S. Institute for Theatre Technology (USITT), 141
University of Florida, 105
University of Virginia, 53
Uptown/downtown, 150
Ushers, 91

Valse, La (ballet), 58
Verdon, Gwen, 64
Vereen, Ben, 57
Victor, Lucia, xx
Virginia Commonwealth University, 7, 28
Virginia Museum of Fine Arts, 49, 53–54
Volunteer work, 109

Walt Disney World, 105–106
Wardrobe master: J. Busheme, 110–116
Webster, Margaret, xx
Wellesley College, 58, 59, 60
Williams, Tennessee, 12
Women in theater, xix–xx
Word-of-mouth advertising, 91
Work in theater: love of, 100, 106, 121; rewards of, xx
Writers (playwrights), xviii, 1–2, 45; J. Bolt, 5–14; rewards of, xx

You're a Good Man, Charlie Brown (play), 20

Zerbe, Anthony, 29
Zipprodt, Patricia, 56–61
Zorba (play), 57, 68